Kissing a cowboy was the last thing in the world she should ever do...

Zach's kiss took Taylor completely by surprise, and yet her arms curled around his neck as if she'd been waiting for this moment all her life. Her body softened against his, feeling his hardness from her chest all the way down.

When he pulled back, she was breathless.

"Wow," he whispered.

"Yeah," she said, her voice shaky and soft.

Then her brain engaged. "You're a cowboy. I can't do this."

He held her gently. "Why not?"

She pushed against his chest, and he let her go. "I won't play second banana to your ranch. I don't like this life. I don't want it."

"I didn't ask you to *marry* me."

"I know." Taylor felt her cheeks heat. "But we have no business kissing."

Taylor watched as Zach walked back to the campsite. She should have been pleased to see him walk away. He was everything she needed to avoid.

If only she could get her head to communicate that message to her heart....

ABOUT THE AUTHOR

A multiple-award-winning author, Jo Leigh began her career in 1975 as a reader for the head of Comedy Development for 20th Century Fox. Since then, she's worked on many movie and television projects, becoming head of development for the McCarron Film Corp. in 1987. She currently resides in Houston, Texas, with her three cats, Coco, Molly and Zeke, and reports that she's smack-dab in the middle of her own personal romance, which makes "research" a real adventure!

Books by Jo Leigh

HARLEQUIN AMERICAN ROMANCE
695—QUICK, FIND A RING!
731—HUSBAND 101
736—DADDY 101
749—IF WISHES WERE...DADDIES

HARLEQUIN TEMPTATION
674—ONE WICKED NIGHT
699—SINGLE SHERIFF SEEKS...

Can't Resist a Cowboy

JO LEIGH

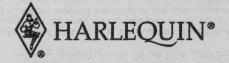

HARLEQUIN®

TORONTO • NEW YORK • LONDON
AMSTERDAM • PARIS • SYDNEY • HAMBURG
STOCKHOLM • ATHENS • TOKYO • MILAN • MADRID
PRAGUE • WARSAW • BUDAPEST • AUCKLAND

To Toni—for O Wyoming

ISBN 0-373-16768-7

CAN'T RESIST A COWBOY

Copyright © 1999 by Jolie Kramer.

This edition published by arrangement with Harlequin Books S.A.

® and TM are trademarks of the publisher. Trademarks indicated with ® are registered in the United States Patent and Trademark Office, the Canadian Trade Marks Office and in other countries.

Printed in U.S.A.

Prologue

Taylor Reed stared at her younger sister with utter astonishment. She'd only been back at the family home for an hour, having driven all the way to Arizona from Houston just to visit with her sisters for the weekend. And they had to hit her with this! The news rocked her to her toes. No wonder Frankie had been acting so peculiarly. Taylor's gaze moved to her other sister. Lori looked just as guilty. So they'd both been in on it!

"It's good news, Taylor," Frankie said, keeping her voice low and calm.

"*Good* news?" Taylor stood up and walked to the kitchen counter. For a moment, she felt as though it was still her mother's kitchen, instead of Lori's. That her mother, in fact, would be sitting at the table as she always had, her hands busy snapping peas or knitting. But as Taylor fixed a new pot of coffee, she knew the feeling of déjà vu was strong because her sisters were carrying on a legacy. A legacy she hated.

She poured water into the pot, not able to still the

slight tremor in her hand. "I can't believe, after all we've been through, after putting up with Dad and his cronies for all those years, that you think marrying a cowboy is good news."

"I'm not marrying a cowboy. I'm marrying Cal."

"What, he's suddenly become an architect?" Taylor came back to the dining room table and sat down again, her gaze falling on an old sampler on the wall. Her mother's work. Lori had kept so much of the past intact.

"No, but he's a lot more than just a cowboy." Frankie reached over and touched Taylor's hand. "He's a wonderful man. If you'd just get to know him a little, you'd see that."

"I don't need to get to know him. I already do." She leaned back, her hand slipping out from beneath Frankie's. "He has a high school education. He works seven days a week, and half the time he doesn't even come home at night. When he does have time off, it's only so he can be in the rodeo. He's broken half the bones in his body, and fully intends to break the rest before he's forty. He's a quiet kind of man, which is appealing from a distance, but in reality means he hasn't got anything of interest to say. He's more at home with his horse than he is with you, which makes sense because his damn horse doesn't care if he misses its birthday or Christmas or any other event that's important. Including the birth of its babies."

Frankie sighed and looked over at Lori. "Talk to her," she said.

Lori shook her head and leaned in to do just that. "You're not being very fair, Taylor. Not all cowboys are like Daddy was."

"Right. Some are drunks, too."

"If that's true, then how come I'm so happy with Jarred?"

Taylor looked at Lori. "Jarred's a decent guy. I never said he wasn't. But that doesn't change the kind of life you've signed up for. You're gonna work yourself to an early grave, just like Mom. And for what? This lousy piece of land we call a ranch? We should have just sold the place and been done with it."

"First of all, I'm not Mom. Second of all, I happen to love this ranch. And I don't mind the work."

"Let's see how you feel about it ten years from now."

"Taylor, you don't understand. I'm happy. Frankie has a chance to be happy. Cowboys are just men. No better, no worse. And Jarred—"

"Where's Jarred now?" Taylor interrupted. "Hmm?"

"You know perfectly well he's in Montana."

"At the rodeo. See? I'm right. Can't you guys see that you've fallen for a myth? A legend? That you're trying to live out the fantasy that ruined Mom's life? Cowboys are not heroes. They never have been, except in the movies."

"Mom's life wasn't ruined," Frankie said softly.

Taylor thought about backing off. Mom was a sensitive subject for Frankie, and she always got upset when Taylor tried to point out the truth. But this was too important. She had to do whatever it took to get her sister to see the mistake she was about to make.

Frankie wasn't strong, like Lori. As far back as she could remember, Taylor had been more like a mother to Frankie than a sister. "Listen, honey," she said as kindly as she could. "For all intents and purposes, Mom raised us alone. At best, she had a part-time husband. But mostly, she just had nothing but hard work and heartache."

"That's not true. Mom loved him. It was you who thought things should be different. Not her."

"Just because a person learns to accept crumbs, doesn't mean they're not crumbs."

Frankie looked at Lori once more, and Taylor could see the silent communication between them. She felt a familiar pang of jealousy. Her two younger sisters had always been so close. They even looked alike, even though there were two years between them. They both had their mother's blond hair and blue eyes; the slim, petite bodies that Taylor had always envied. And while Frankie looked to Taylor for advice, she went to Lori for friendship.

Lori nodded ever so slightly at Frankie, confirming Taylor's impression that this wasn't a spur-of-the-moment discussion. Then she turned to Taylor. "Are you going to support her in this?"

"I don't see how I can. Not in good conscience. Not when I know it's going to make her miserable."

"It's not fair," Frankie said. "You don't even know Cal. You don't know the first thing about him."

"Is that my fault? You've hardly mentioned him to me. I don't even know how you met him."

Frankie smiled. "I met him at the hotel last summer, when I was waitressing. He used to come by to eat Sunday dinners. I noticed him right off. God, he was so handsome."

"Handsome?" Taylor said, shaking her head. "That's the worst reason in the world to fall in love with someone."

"That's not why I fell in love," Frankie said. "Although it didn't hurt."

"So what else makes him so darn special?"

"It won't do me any good to tell you," Frankie said, leaning forward. "You have to see that for yourself."

"And how am I supposed to do that?"

"He's invited you to come up to the ranch where he's working this summer. He's even offered to pay your way."

"Don't be silly."

"It's true," Lori said. "For your information, Cal, who you think is some insensitive dumb ox, is quite concerned that you won't give Frankie your blessing. He doesn't want that. And he's willing to put his money where his mouth is."

"Well, it's ridiculous."

"Why? What will it hurt you to go and see?"

"First, because I'd rather poke my eye out with a

stick than spend time on a ranch. Second, because it's not going to make any difference.''

"I've never known you to back away from a challenge, Taylor," Lori said. "Or to be so unfair about something so important."

"So what if I go, and I still think she's making a mistake?"

"Then I'll listen." Frankie caught her gaze and held it. "I won't promise to call off the engagement, but I'll really think about it. You know how much I respect you, Taylor. Your good wishes mean a great deal to me. I know it's not the way you want to spend your vacation, but I hope you'll consider it."

"Didn't you just tell us that you didn't know what you were going to do with your time off?" Lori asked.

"And didn't you also say that you wanted to get away from the city?"

Taylor studied her little sisters while she weighed her options. If she didn't go, Frankie and Lori would both be terribly upset, and with their mother so recently gone, she didn't want that. They were family, and that mattered. She had no doubt that being on the ranch would just confirm her beliefs, but she wanted Frankie to see that she'd gone with an open mind. How could she prove that?

A glimmer of an idea popped into her head. She got up and went to the counter again and poured herself a cup of the fresh brew. Maybe... Could she pull it off? An exposé. For the newspaper. The truth about cowboys. The real skinny. Showing everyone, including

Frankie, that the myth of the cowboy was just that. A myth.

"Well?"

She came back to the table and sat down, purposefully hiding her excitement at her plan. "Wyoming, huh?" she asked.

"It's gorgeous there, Taylor," Frankie said, unable to disguise the hopefulness in her voice. "God's country."

"I haven't ridden in years, you know."

"And you miss it," Lori said.

Taylor sighed. "All right."

Frankie and Lori exchanged excited glances. "You'll really give him a chance?" Frankie asked.

"You'll stay for the full two weeks?" Lori asked.

"Two weeks? No way!"

"Come on, Taylor," Frankie said. "Don't back out now. Two measly little weeks. It's barely enough time to get to know Cal as it is."

"We'll see," she said. "I had thought about going to Washington. There's an important vote coming up in the Senate—"

"I don't believe you!" Lori said. "This is supposed to be a vacation. Not work. You said yourself that you needed a break from that newspaper of yours."

"I didn't say that. Quentin said that."

"Well? Maybe your editor is onto something."

Taylor sighed again. This could be perfect. She could show Quentin that she didn't need a vacation. That she could still find a story, even on vacation.

"So, you'll go?" Frankie asked again.

She took a deep breath and let it out slowly. "I'll give it my best shot," she said. Now all she had to do was figure out how to get her story, get it printed, and prove once and for all that cowboys and marriage didn't mix. After all, Frankie's future was at stake.

Chapter One

Taylor gaped as she put her suitcase and backpack down on the dirt road. She couldn't help it. The view in front of her quite simply took her breath away.

Directly ahead was a sprawling ranch house, beautiful in its own right, but dwarfed by the background. Nothing could compete with the Grand Tetons. White capped, green carpeted, the mountains awed her. Pictures didn't do them justice. Neither did adjectives. New words needed to be invented exclusively for this sight.

She glanced to her left, at the cloud of dust the taxicab was leaving in its wake, but something wasn't right about it. Something…

Just then, through the billowing cloud, she saw him. A cowboy on horseback, riding straight toward her. In a flash, she seemed to go back in time. She was ten, and her father was riding up the long road home, his horse's hooves mesmerizing her with a rhythm that sank into her very bones.

She studied the rider, looking for Jack Reed, but it

wasn't him, of course. It was just another cowboy. With the mountains behind him, he looked like Gary Cooper or John Wayne. Every movie cowboy she'd ever seen. His Stetson low on his forehead, his duster flapping around him like wings, he seemed the very essence of a hero, riding in to save the day.

She knew better. She'd waited for heroes all her life, but they never rode in. They didn't exist outside the movie theaters. Every cowboy she knew was nothing but trouble. Some more than others.

This was her chance to tell the truth. To tell all those women who fantasized about gunslingers and cowpokes who their idols really were. And the cowboy coming straight at her was a perfect example. From here, he looked strong, self-assured, capable of handling any emergency, from birthing a calf to stringing up cattle rustlers. The only thing missing was the music from *The Magnificent Seven*.

But when he got closer, she'd see that it was all a facade. He'd be dusty—probably ripe—with chapped hands and face. Hard and taciturn, his silence not a mark of deep thought, but a result of having nothing upstairs to think with. He'd prefer dealing with cows, mostly because they rarely spoke. He'd have no social skills, except, of course, the ever-popular peeing out the campfire.

Or it could be worse. He might not have any outward signs of his true nature. He might be clean and handsome, and be able to talk the birds out of the trees. Those cowboys were the most dangerous. *That* she knew from personal experience. Because what those cowboys could do was make a girl think she'd found a real hero, when all she'd found was heartache on a horse.

The rider grew nearer, and clearer. Even from this distance she could see he was a cowboy of the second kind. Handsome. There might be a flaw when she got close up, but she doubted it. He slowed his horse, and she shifted her gaze to the animal. It was a beauty. A quarter-horse, if she wasn't mistaken. Seal brown, with white stockings.

The horse pulled up ten feet from her, and she got a good look at the rider.

Her first impulse was to run. She could feel her heart hammer like pounding hooves in her chest, and her hands clenched in tight fists. She'd only known this feeling once before. It had signaled the beginning of the worst episode in her life. But this was a stranger—a tall stranger who looked down at her with a scowl that made her take a step back.

"You the reporter?" he asked.

"Yes." She took a deep breath and held her hand out. "Taylor Reed."

He didn't bother to take her hand. He just kept staring at her with accusing eyes.

"I assume you're Zach Baldwin?" she asked, lowering her hand with as much dignity as she could muster. She straightened her shoulders, trying hard not to feel intimidated by his stern gaze.

"This is my ranch," he said coolly.

Even though he was sitting on his horse, she could see that he was tall and lean and muscular. One of those men with deceptive strength, rock hard and weather-beaten. His dark thick hair curled over his collar. Her attention was snagged by a lock of hair falling across his forehead. She could just imagine the many feminine fingers that had brushed that hair back.

She continued to catalog his face, concentrating as hard as she could, even though she knew he didn't like her perusal. But she was a reporter and she wanted to remember her first impression. To recreate it exactly. Maybe then she could figure out why...

"I said, this is my ranch."

She heard him. But she didn't rush. Or acknowledge his bark. She just took him in, one chiseled feature at a time. Firm jaw, patrician nose, and of course, his eyes. They were actually gray. Not hazel. Gray.

He was the quintessential cowboy, all right. Even with that scowl on his face, she recognized that he embodied all the mythology—quiet, strong, capable, loyal and forthright. A regular boy scout with sex appeal.

Now, all she had to do was figure out which kind of cowboy he was. Good at riding, but not writing? Able to whisper to horses, but not to read books that didn't have pictures? Or was he a sweet-talking snake charmer? A man who understood the power of his appeal, and used it to his every advantage?

He shifted in his saddle, looking a bit more exasperated than he had two minutes ago. That was better.

She felt the knot in her stomach start to unclench. If there was one thing she knew how to do, it was exasperate a man. For the first time since he'd ridden up, she felt as if she were on firm ground.

"I don't know what you said to Pearl to get her to ask you out here, Ms. Reed," he said, "but frankly, I don't like it. I don't like reporters and I don't like strangers on my spread."

"Well, thank you for being so straightforward, Mr. Baldwin. I'll keep that in mind. Now, perhaps you'll forgive me if I leave this warm, fuzzy welcome. I have an appointment to keep."

She picked up her luggage and started walking to the house. Why hadn't Frankie told her about her charming host? And why did it bother her so much to think about him watching her as she walked away?

Then she heard the soft click of his tongue, and the unmistakable sound of a horse's hoof on dirt. He followed her, keeping a good ten feet behind, but it was quite disconcerting to know he was there.

"Can you ride?" he asked, his voice still stern and angry.

She nodded.

"Ever handled cattle?"

She glanced back at him. "A little."

He pushed back that single lock of hair that had fallen across his forehead. "This isn't a dude ranch."

"I'm aware of that. And please don't worry. I have no intention of getting in the way."

He nodded, then rode up next to her, tall in the saddle.

"What are your intentions?" he asked, leading her across the gravel driveway to the steps of the big house. Once there, he dismounted and let the reins drop to the ground. The horse stood still.

"I'm here to get to know one of your ranch hands," she said. "Cal. He's intending to marry my sister."

"I know that part. What else?"

"Pardon?"

"I said, what else? You can't be here just to meet Cal. You could do that over dinner."

"I'm also here on assignment," she said. "I'm doing an article for the newspaper I work for. About modern ranching."

He studied her for a long moment, cataloging her features as intensely as she'd cataloged his just a few moments ago. She didn't like being on this end so much. She wondered if he was going to tell her to leave. She also wondered if leaving wasn't such a bad idea. There was a lot about Zach Baldwin that made her uncomfortable. He reminded her too much of men she'd encountered growing up.

"Pearl asked you here," he said, finally. "So you can stay, but I'll tell you now, you get in the way, you distract any of my hands, and that's it. You're gone." Then, without waiting for her to respond, he turned and walked inside.

She knew right then that it would take a team of wild horses to get her off this ranch before her two weeks were up. This man, this rude cowboy, was the perfect subject for her article. She was going to expose Zach Baldwin to the world. And she was going to show Frankie just how big a mistake it would be for her to walk down the aisle with a cowboy.

She transferred her suitcase to her other hand, then went through the open front door.

She liked the house the moment she crossed the threshold. It was a very large ranch home, made of native wood. The first thing she noticed was the fireplace that nearly covered one wall, and the rich dark leather furniture that looked comfortable enough to sleep in.

Zach stood by the fireplace, evidently waiting for her. She started toward him, and he led her through an enormous dining room, down a hallway that had portraits lining the walls, then to a staircase.

As he started climbing ahead of her, she couldn't help but notice the way his jeans fit. Well worn, with a small patch just above the right pocket, they did very little to hide the fine specimen underneath. She had to admit, that was one thing about cowboys she did like. The rear view. Preferably when they were walking out of her life.

She reached the second floor and followed Zach past a bathroom, a closed door, and then to a guest bedroom where he waited while she put down her suitcase. The room wasn't large, but it was tastefully decorated and looked quite comfortable. The queen-size bed had a lovely quilt on it, the oak dresser was adequate for her needs. There was even a small desk in the corner, next to the bookcase. It would be easy to set up her laptop and write here.

"The towels are in the bathroom, and sheets are in the closet. We eat three times a day, at five-thirty, noon and six. You'll find Pearl in the kitchen if you need anything."

"What about you?"

"Me?"

"Yes. And Cal. Where will I find you?"

He sighed, looked down at the floor for a minute, then back up at her. "I'll be in the barn out back. I'll see if I can round up Cal for you."

"Thank you."

He kind of nodded, then turned and walked out of the room. But she wasn't surprised about that. She was never surprised when cowboys were abrupt.

She sat on the edge of the bed and looked at the neatly arranged books on the shelf. They were an eclectic bunch. A few Reader's Digest condensed novels, some paperback romances and mysteries, and then some nonfiction on horse husbandry. She wondered who stacked the shelves. Probably Pearl.

Frankie had told her more about Pearl than about her nephew Zach. She was in her mid-sixties, but from what Frankie said, she had the energy of two twenty-year-olds. She did most of the cooking by herself and she ran the household.

Taylor looked forward to meeting her, and not just because Frankie spoke so highly of her. Pearl would know a thing or two about cowboys. She'd lived with them for her whole life. Taylor was sure to get some terrific insights into what made most cowboys so...so insufferable.

Well, she'd better get on with it. She lifted her big suitcase to the bed, and started unpacking. Her thoughts weren't on closet space though. They were on her article, and the cowboy she was going to base it on. Zach Baldwin.

ZACH MOUNTED HIS HORSE, and headed off toward the stables. He didn't hurry, even though Charlie was probably chomping at the bit to go over the cattle-drive schedule. Zach was more concerned with the woman upstairs. He still couldn't believe Pearl would go and do a thing like inviting her without talking to him. But she'd said it was her home too, and that she had every right to invite whomever she pleased. Which was true, but dammit, Pearl knew how he felt about having women here. And this woman spelled trouble in any number of ways.

First, she was entirely too attractive. Second, she was going to write about him and his men. He hated all that sappy junk about the noble cowboy. As far as he was concerned, cowboys weren't any more noble than anyone else. It was a job, pure and simple. One he loved, but he didn't glamorize it. She would, though. He just felt it.

The way she'd looked at him, he could already tell that she'd gotten that greenhorn crush. Not that he took it personally. It was the horse, the hat, the clothes, the ranch. Taylor Reed had just succumbed to Wyoming Fever, that's all. It had happened before, especially with the tourists in town. He just hoped she'd get over it before she left. Maybe then she'd write a sensible article, one that dealt with the real issues of modern ranching. Not some twaddle about the moon and wind and the brave cowboys who stood for honor and decent values.

But it was that first thing that worried him most. A woman like that could make a man forget what he was doing. Which could lead to mistakes. Dangerous mistakes.

The boys that worked for him were good kids for the most part. Hard workers. They knew the ranch, and they took care of business. But he'd seen what could happen when pretty girls came to the ranch. And Taylor wasn't just pretty. She was a beauty.

She reminded him of Lauren Bacall—in *Key Largo*. Her hair was a little darker, had a little more red, but it was long, and curled under, just like Bacall's. Her face had that delicate heart shape, with the same smoky eyes. She was tall and slender. Almost mysterious. And the boys would fall all over themselves to impress her. Which would mess up his schedule, if he was lucky. If he wasn't, his schedule would be the *least* of his problems.

He clicked his tongue, which was enough for Falcon to pick up his pace. He went into an easy lope, anxious to get back to his stall and alfalfa.

The next two weeks were going to be hard on everyone. They had a lot of fence to repair, a lot of cows
to round up. The men were already distracted by the
prospect of the drive to the high pasture. Adding Reed
to the pot was asking for trouble.

He rode over the crest and headed straight for the
barn. He could see Charlie standing by the great door.
Jesse and Tony were in the feeding pen, taking care
of the hogs, and Little Danny was over by the ranch
office. He didn't see Big Danny. Maybe he was already off to the store.

There were too many things going on to worry about
that woman. Maybe there was a way to keep her out
of trouble. She was here to write about real ranch life,
so that's what he'd give her. Real, unadulterated ranch
life. The hard-core stuff the men hated, but learned to
do without complaint. Mucking out the stables. Fixing
the fences at the back end of the ranch. Slopping the
hogs. Cleaning the horses' hooves. It wouldn't make
for a very romantic article, that's for sure. Maybe she'd
see that she was barking up the wrong tree, and head
out.

And he'd better take charge of her himself. At least
he wouldn't get all bent out of shape over her being
pretty. Sure, he appreciated her looks, but that didn't
mean he had to do anything about it. Especially not
now. Not with the drive so near.

Ah, dammit, he just wished she hadn't come. It had
been a long while since he'd had to deal with a woman
like her. Especially here, on his place. He preferred to

meet women from town who didn't intend to interfere with his life.

This one, this Taylor Reed, had all the earmarks, all right. He remembered the look she'd given him. The challenge that was in her eyes. The curiosity. Well, that was just too bad. She wasn't going to get what she wanted. If she didn't like it, she could go right back to wherever she came from. Probably someplace like New York. Or Boston. Some big city where they didn't understand the first thing about working the land.

He slowed Falcon down as they approached the barn. Charlie waved at him. Zach dismounted as soon as he was at the big gate.

"Where the hell you been?" Charlie asked. "I can't stand around here all day waiting, you know."

Zach nodded at his foreman while he uncinched Falcon's saddle and took it off. He put the saddle and blanket on the fence, then ran a hand down the horse's chest. He hadn't worked up too much of a sweat. Zach would let him eat a bit now, and then brush him down after he finished with Charlie.

He took hold of the reins and led Falcon into the stable, down to his stall. Charlie walked with them, but he didn't say anything. One thing life on a ranch taught a man was patience. Although Charlie wasn't as good at it as some. When things weren't going his way, he tended to grind his teeth. He was grinding them now.

"Why don't you start by telling me what Doc Foster

had to say," Zach said, taking the reins off Falcon. "Then we'll head over to the office."

He listened as Charlie brought him up to date, but his gaze wandered over the horses that were still in their stalls. Once he got to Paladin, he stopped short. Now, that was an interesting idea. That woman said she'd ridden. He'd take her at her word. He didn't think Paladin would hurt her—just make her a little...uncomfortable.

"Dangit, boy, you heard one word I said?"

Zach turned his attention to Charlie, and cursed. "It's that reporter woman."

"The one who's coming to check Cal out? What about her?"

"She's here. And she wants to check out more than Cal. She wants to learn all about ranch life for some article."

"Give her to Big Danny. He'll show her around. And he knows how to keep her away from the boys."

Zach shook his head. "Nope. Won't work."

"Why not?"

"You remember that gal from San Antonio?"

Charlie nodded slowly, frowning.

"This one's prettier. Big Danny won't be able to keep the boys away, even if he uses his shotgun."

The expletive Charlie spat out said it all. "So what are we gonna do with her?"

"I'm gonna keep her with me. It's safer that way."

Charlie's brow went up. "And what makes you immune? I seen what happened with you and that gal from San Antonio. As I recall, you came away from that mighty bruised and beaten.''

''This one isn't my type.''

''Is she breathing?''

Zach nodded.

''Then she's your type.''

''Very funny. I'm telling you, I'll take care of it.''

Charlie crossed his arms over his ample belly. ''I wouldn't be so sure, young Zachary. Seems to me it's been a long time since you got in a tangle over a woman.''

''Forget it. It won't happen.''

''Why not? You say she's a looker.''

''She's also a city gal. She sits in an office all day. As I said, not my type.''

''A man can make a fool of himself over a city gal just as easy as a country gal.''

Zach crossed his arms over his chest. ''Not me,'' he said. ''I learned my lesson. Every time a woman sets foot on this ranch, something goes wrong.''

''I don't know. Maybe that's all finished with.''

''That kind of bad luck doesn't get finished with.''

''Now, come on, Zach. It's been quite a while since anyone got hurt out here.''

''Right. And I want to keep it that way. Surest way of doing that is to keep the boys busy. Keep their minds on the job, not on some woman reporter's backside.''

Charlie walked over to Paladin and took a look at his back leg for a moment. When he stood up again, he didn't seem worried, so Zach let it go. But an instant later, the concern on Charlie's face was back—only this time it wasn't the horse he studied.

"Zach, when's the last time you took a lady out to dinner?" he asked finally.

Zach didn't like where this was headed. "Don't you have a schedule you want to go over?"

"Answer my question, son. When's the last time you went out on a date? And poker at Mary Lou's doesn't count."

"I've been out."

"With a woman."

"Dammit, Charlie. Can we just get to work?"

"It ain't natural, is what I think. A man your age, you should be thinking about settling down. Having kids."

"I don't need to settle down. And I got kids. Ten boys, and they all work for me."

"Those boys aren't here for good, buddy, and I hate to tell you, but you're not getting any younger."

"Look who's talking! You're almost forty-five, and I don't see you with a wife and kids."

"I'm not happy about that. If I had to do it again, I would do it different. Sometimes I wonder what it would have been like to have someone to confide in besides my horse."

"Come on, you've always told me that no man can be truly free if he's married."

"Since when do you listen to me? I'm just on old fool, and you know it. A lonely old fool."

Zach turned to Falcon and petted the animal's strong neck. It made him uncomfortable to hear Charlie talk like that. It was all *her* fault. She hadn't been here an hour, and she was already messing things up.

The nagging feeling was back in the pit of his stomach. Taylor Reed was trouble, all right. Now he was sure of it. Trouble with a capital *T*.

Chapter Two

Taylor found her way to the kitchen by following the heavenly smells. At the door she got a first look at Zach's aunt Pearl. She could see right away that Zach's good looks were a family trait. Pearl wasn't as tall as Taylor, but close. Trim in jeans and a western blouse, with silver hair cut in a short curly bob, she looked as though she could handle a lot more than just cooking for the ranch hands. Given her nephew's temperament, that made sense.

Pearl turned from the pot on the stove, as Taylor walked into the kitchen. "Pearl?"

The older woman gave her an appraising look, then smiled. "You must be Taylor."

"Guilty," Taylor said, holding out her hand.

Pearl shook it with surprising vigor. "Nice to have you here. Have you found your room yet?"

Taylor nodded. "Zach took me up."

"So you've met him, have you?"

"Yep. I don't think he's very enthusiastic about me being here."

"I see you're a master of understatement. Well, now that I get a look at you, I can see his point. You're going to cause a stir, that's for sure."

"What do you mean?"

Pearl hesitated. "You want some coffee?"

"Sure."

Taylor waited while Pearl got down a couple of mugs, and as she poured them each a cup, Taylor looked around the spacious kitchen. There were two ovens, a six-burner stove upon which two pots were boiling, a couple of microwaves, and if she wasn't mistaken, the fridge was one of those zero-degree jobs. The whole huge room was immaculate, and she especially liked the big island. It had a built-in sink, and down the side there were drawers for flour and potatoes and onions.

Pearl grabbed both cups and lead her to a breakfast nook at the far end of the kitchen. "Sit down. You want milk or sugar?"

Taylor nodded, and after Pearl put down the mugs, she got the creamer and the sugar bowl and brought them both with her. Finally, Pearl slid in across from her. "I can see some of Frankie in you."

"Really? It's our other sister, Lori, who looks like Frankie."

"So who do you take after? Your mother or father?"

"My father, but only in the looks department, thank goodness."

Pearl looked a little puzzled. "Frankie told me some

stories about your dad. She seemed proud of his rodeo ribbons."

"Yeah, he did win plenty of those. Tell me, how did you and Frankie meet?"

"I play cards at the hotel where she worked over the summer. That's where she met Cal, too."

"If you don't mind, I'd like to ask you some questions about him."

"I don't mind at all. I'll do what I can to help Frankie and Cal. I think they're a good match."

Taylor looked down, holding back a biting comment. She didn't want to start her stay here with an argument. And she certainly didn't want to appear as if she'd already made up her mind about Cowboy Cal. Maybe she should wait until she met him before hearing Pearl's opinions.

She moved her gaze back up, deciding a little sidestepping was in order. "You were saying something about me causing a stir?"

The older woman sipped her coffee, then nodded. "There are a lot of young men here on the ranch. Mostly in their late teens or early twenties. More than a few of them have had some problems in school, or with the law. Nothing too serious. Mostly running with the wrong kids, or discipline issues. Zach makes it a point to hire boys who need a guiding hand and some hard work to straighten them out."

Taylor swallowed her coffee while she grappled with this interesting piece of information. Could it be that Zach was a cowboy with a conscience? With a sense of duty to his community? Then she thought about her father, and how kind he was to every stray ranch hand and drunk he ran into, mostly at the expense of his wife and kids. It made sense that Zach would want to help some local boys. Train 'em early and train 'em right. "So why is my visit here a problem?"

"It's not you, Taylor. It's women."

"He has a thing against women?" A picture of Zach was slowly forming. Not only was he invested in keeping the wheels of his old boys' network greased and running, he was also a misogynist. *Great.* This was going to be a really swell vacation.

Pearl smiled. "No, he doesn't have a problem with women in general. Matter of fact, I happen to know he likes women very much. He just doesn't like women here on the ranch."

"Why not?"

"Now that's a long story. One I think you'll want to hear direct from the horse's mouth."

From the sound of Pearl's voice, Taylor was pretty sure she wasn't going to get any more information about Zach and his peculiarities from her. Not yet, at least. But she wasn't a journalist for nothing. She'd bide her time and find out all she needed to know. "Fair enough," Taylor said. "But let me get this straight—you're the only woman here?"

"Yep. Been that way for about five years."

"That must be difficult for you."

She shook her head. "Not really. I have my friends,

and three nights a week I go out to the Jackson Hole community center. I take Tai Chi, and I play bridge over at the hotel. I get my fill of feminine gossip there.''

"So I guess I won't quite blend in, huh?''

"No, sweetie. Not with your looks. I'd say you're going to be quite a distraction.''

"If you don't mind my asking, why did you agree to have me come? I know Frankie told you I was a female.''

"I did it for her. For Frankie.''

"I assume she told you everything?''

"She said you were here to get to know Cal. That you're against them getting married.''

"And you side with her?''

"That I do. I know Cal. He's a good boy. He had some rough times—a little trouble with truancy when he was in school—but that wasn't his fault. His father left him when he was three, and his mother had more than a casual friendship with the bottle. He didn't have it easy, but since he's been here, he's worked hard, and he shows every sign of being a fine man. You'll see.''

Taylor looked at her fingers circling the coffee mug. "I hope so.''

"Now, didn't Frankie say you were interested in politics?''

"Yes, that's right. I'm actually waiting to hear about an assignment in Washington. If I'm lucky, I'll be go-

ing there after I leave here to cover the congressional
hearings on education.''

"So this is a vacation?''

"In a way. I'm doing a piece for my paper on the
new cowboy, so it's a busman's holiday.''

Pearl smiled enigmatically. "I have a hunch you'll
find this assignment just as interesting as a congressional hearing.''

Taylor took a sip of coffee. "I hope you're right,''
she said. "I'd better get out there. I want to go intro-
duce myself to Cal. And I have a feeling I'd better
show your nephew that I plan to blend right in.''

"Good luck on that one,'' Pearl said. "About
Zach...''

"Yes?''

"He can be gruff sometimes, but he doesn't have a
mean bone in his body.''

"I see,'' she said, wondering how much of that
statement was true, and how much wishful thinking.
"And thanks. For having me here. For arranging for
me to go on the cattle drive. I just know it's going to
make a great story.''

"I think it's going to be quite an adventure,'' Pearl
said.

"I can see why Frankie wanted me to meet you.''

"I just hope when she and Cal get married they
choose to make their home up here. She's a sweet girl,
and I know the hotel would like to hire her for more
than just the summer.''

"I'll tell her you said so.'' Taylor scooted out of

the booth and pointed out the kitchen door. "That way?"

Pearl nodded. "Not the sliding glass door. That leads to the deck and the hot tub. You want the second door. You'll see the barn as soon as you're outside."

"Will you let me know if there's anything I can do to help you?"

"That I will."

Taylor smiled once more, and headed out—to the barn and another meeting with Zach. She had to admit that she was surprised at Pearl's description of him. But then, Pearl was family, and as Taylor knew too well, family had a way of seeing what they wanted to, instead of what was there.

ZACH HEARD Big Danny's low whistle, and knew that Taylor was on her way. Sure enough, when he looked up at the house, he could see her walking purposefully down the path straight at him.

He took his time watching her. The sway of her hips, the way her hair moved on her shoulders. Maybe he *had* been too long without a woman. Without the feel of a female in his bed.

His gaze trailed down her body, and he had no trouble at all imagining what was underneath that T-shirt and those tight jeans. She was as young and lithe as a thoroughbred colt. And he got the feeling she'd be just as lively.

He heard another whistle, but when he looked around he couldn't find the culprit. The wolf call had cleared his head, though. It got his mind off things he shouldn't be thinking. What he needed now was to keep his wits about him.

Zach had seen what happened when two wild stallions got wind of a female in heat. They fought, and kept on fighting, until the strongest subdued or killed his rival. One thing about human females—they were always in heat. And he didn't doubt for a moment that his young men would fight as fiercely as any stallion. If they got the chance. Which he wasn't going to give them.

As far as this ranch went, he was the alpha male, and there wasn't a boy or man here who was going to challenge that position. Anyone who did would be out of here so fast, they'd get motion sickness.

"Well, hell, Zach," Charlie said, wiping his brow with his shirtsleeve as she approached. "She *is* prettier than that gal from San Antonio."

"I told you."

"What are you gonna do about it?"

"Keep her with me. That's all I can do."

"It's not going to be enough."

"It will if we make sure it is." Zach turned to the foreman. "We're gonna have to be on our toes, Charlie."

"I don't know, Zach. She's awful pretty. And we've got ten red-blooded, hard-working boys out here. How are we supposed to keep them away from her on the cattle drive?"

"What are you talking about? She'll be long gone by then."

"Not according to Pearl."

Zach stared at Charlie, waiting for him to break into a grin. But he didn't. "I don't care what Pearl said. I'm not taking that female on the cattle drive."

"Why not?"

Zach spun around at the sound of her voice, to see the female in question right behind him. "You're just not going. That's all."

"But that's why I'm here. To write about the drive. It's pretty useless for me to have come all this way if I can't go with you."

"Sorry about that."

Charlie coughed and then held his hand out to Taylor. "Charlie Ridgeway, ma'am. I'm the foreman here on the ranch."

"Nice to meet you," she said, taking his big hand in hers. When she let go, she crossed her arms and zeroed in on Zach again. His gaze fell to her bosom. He could see her curves beneath her T-shirt. Those curves were enough of a reason for him to stand his ground.

"Is it because you don't think I can ride?"

"I'm sure you can. Just not the kind of riding you'd have to do on a drive. It's eighteen hours a day on a saddle."

"And you don't think I can do that."

"Frankly, I don't know what you can do, although I doubt very much if you even have an idea of the kind of work it takes to drive eight hundred head all the way to the high pasture. But it doesn't matter. 'Cause you aren't going."

She sighed, raising those curves then letting them settle. He lifted his gaze to her face. She looked determined. Not that any amount of determination on her part was going to change his mind.

"What if I prove it to you?"

"Prove what?"

"That I won't get in the way. That I can handle myself on the drive."

He smiled, although he didn't find anything humorous about the situation. "Look, Ms. Reed. We're leaving next Monday. You have any idea how much work I have to do before we head out?"

Taylor stared straight at him. "You have to prepare the remuda and pick out all the horses. You have to make sure the chuck wagon and equipment are all packed. I imagine you're wagon boss, and that you have a full complement of cowhands, but since I gather they're on the young side, you're going to want to check out their equipment, too. I also imagine you need to check the weather, and make sure you've mapped out the campsites correctly. And then, of course, there's the veterinary supplies, the inoculations and such. Am I getting close?"

Zach heard Charlie's muffled chuckle. He decided to ignore that. "Learning about what goes on during a drive, and *working* on a drive are two different things."

"Granted. But I assure you, I know what I'm doing."

"Where are you from, anyway?"

"I was born and raised in Arizona."

"I thought Pearl said you lived in the city."

"I live in Houston now."

"But you grew up on a ranch?"

"Yep."

"How many head?"

"Not many," she said, still standing up to him, her gaze never leaving his face. "But I've ridden since I was three. I've gone on the spring roundup since I was ten. I've trained cutting horses, and I've ridden in the rodeo. I can handle it."

Zach kicked at a rock, then looked to his right. Three boys—Jesse, Little Danny and Pete—stood there like the Three Stooges, just staring. At her. Zach turned to face them, and they started to move back straight away. "You boys don't have enough work to do? I can always find you more."

"No, sir," Little Danny said. "We're just on our way."

"Well then get."

"Yes, sir," Pete said as he walked backwards toward the barn. He wasn't looking at Zach, though. He was still staring at Taylor. Then his heel hit on something, and he peddled backward. His arms couldn't do the job, and he landed on the ground with a *thump*.

It was just as Zach had suspected. The woman hadn't been here ten minutes, and already the boys were hurting themselves, staring and showing off. She'd be a disaster on the drive. No one would get any work done. And out on the range, there weren't any local doctors. Someone could get killed.

He turned to face Taylor again, and noticed that she wasn't paying attention to Pete. Her focus was on him. He recognized the look she gave him. He'd grown used to seeing that look on Pearl's face when she was setting out to make his life miserable.

"So?" she asked. "What can I do to prove to you that I can help on this drive?"

He didn't want to have the standoff right here. Not when the boys were so close. There was no way she was going to go with him, so it really didn't matter what he told her. "I have to go ride some bog. Why don't we get you set up with a horse, and you can come with me."

"I'd like to meet Cal first, if I could."

"He's working. You can meet with him when we get back."

She looked troubled for a moment, then nodded. "I need to go get my hat and gloves," she said. "I'll be right back." Before she left, she smiled at Charlie. "Nice meeting you," she said.

Charlie grinned back at her, which irritated Zach, but he'd look like a jerk if he told Charlie not to smile at her.

"Real pleasure to have you here," Charlie said. "I'm looking forward to working with you."

Taylor's smile widened as she looked back at Zach. Was that triumph he saw in her eyes?

She didn't stick around long enough for him to be sure, just took off up the hill. Zach watched her go. She hurried, and the view of her running up the crest to the house was damn good. Not to mention distracting.

"Seems to me like she'll make a fine addition to the staff," Charlie said.

Zach opened his mouth to give Charlie what for, but then he closed it again. No use getting into an argument when he held all the cards.

"I was thinking of giving her Zoro," Charlie said after a bit.

Zach knew that Zoro would be a good horse for Taylor. But he wasn't interested in making a match. "Paladin," he said.

"What? That horse isn't fit for anyone but the rough string rider."

"She said she could ride. We'll find out."

Charlie shrugged. "It's your ranch."

"That's right," Zach said. "My ranch, and my rules."

Charlie studied him for a long spell. "How'd you like to make a little wager," he said, finally.

"On what?"

"On her."

"What exactly?"

"That she rides with us on the drive."

"I told you—"

"I know what you told me. So you shouldn't be worried about the bet, right?"

Zach shook his head. The man didn't get it. Even

after all the years he'd been foreman. Just because Pearl wanted her way didn't mean she was going to *get* her way. Not when it came to the safety of his men. "How much?"

"A hundred."

"I'm telling you, Charlie. You're wasting your money."

"You let me worry about that. Is it a deal?"

Zach stuck out his hand. "It's a deal. But you're a fool."

Charlie grinned. "We'll see who's the fool come next Monday."

"I swear, old man. You're going plumb senile, you know that?"

"Call me names all you want. I'm still gonna be spending your hundred dollars on wine, women and song... I'm going over to the tack room and go over the equipment," he added. "See you at dinner."

Zach nodded, his gaze still on the back door of the house. Another few seconds went by, and he let the sounds around him tell him what was going on. The dogs were barking, probably at the chickens. Big Danny was back, working on an engine. The farrier was in the barn, hammering on some shoes. He was used to the sounds around him. Masculine. Rough. He didn't encourage cursing, but he understood it. Then the back door opened, and she came out. She headed toward him, the cowboy hat she'd fetched on her head. Now that *she* was here, the sounds, along with every-thing else, were going to change. Her voice was soft and silky. And there was no room for soft and silky on his ranch—or in his life.

It wasn't going to be easy, he realized. Not when she made him this aware of how much he missed being with a woman. He recognized his needs, and he normally took care of them, but not here on the ranch, and not while he was preparing for a roundup or a drive. This was a time of extreme physical labor. Even more than he normally faced. He needed his strength, his focus and his energy to be concentrated on one thing, and one thing only: making sure the men and the cattle made it up to the high pasture safe and sound.

It wasn't going to work. There were too many compelling reasons to get her off the ranch. He'd take her out with him today. This time of the year, a few head would get bogged down in the mud near the water holes. He or the boys had gone out every day for the past week, and they'd found at least one critter stuck each day.

It would be a good test for her. He'd watch her saddle up, and try to handle Paladin. Then, if she made it that far, he'd stand back and watch her try and figure out how to get a Hereford cow out of mud as thick as quicksand.

By the time he brought her back to the house for dinner, she'd be begging him to take her back to town. And then he wouldn't think about those curves of hers, ever again.

Chapter Three

Taylor tried to appear casual as she headed back to the barn. But it was hard to keep her excitement hidden. This article was going to be fantastic! The more she learned about Zach, the more certain she became that he was the embodiment of everything that was wrong with cowboys. Arrogant, sexist, pigheaded and chauvinistic. All contained in a movie-idol package that would look terrific on page one. Maybe she shouldn't give this to the *Chronicle*. Maybe she should do it for *Cosmo* instead.

Her gaze traveled over the man, lingering at his broad shoulders and tight little hips. Such a beautiful specimen. Which was the problem of course. How were women to know that such a painful gift was wrapped so well?

She saw him give her another of his critical once-overs, his frown deepening the closer she got to him. He didn't say anything. He just stuck his hand in his right pocket. "You say you can ride?" Zach asked after another uncomfortable moment.

"Yes, I can."

"Okay, then," he said, turning toward the stable. "I've got just the animal for you."

She didn't much care for his tone. That arrogance again, as if being a woman and riding well were mutually exclusive. It was like going back in time to a past that held no nostalgia for her. Growing up at the ranch, she'd often been dismissed, told she couldn't go, she couldn't try, she shouldn't want—all because she didn't have the right plumbing. She remembered too well her father's criticism about the way she rode, the way she handled cattle. And how he made her feel as if she'd never do anything right.

What Mr. High-and-Mighty Zach didn't realize was that his disdain—the disdain of all the men who'd ever told her "no"—made her stronger. Made her more determined than ever. So let him treat her like a helpless deficient. His comeuppance would be all the sweeter.

"This way," he said, pointing to a stall at the back of the stable.

Taylor looked around to see stall after stall, most of them empty. She knew it was a large spread, but she was amazed at the size of the place.

Zach must have done something right. It was expensive to maintain a place like this. It took excellent management skills as well as good horse sense. But then, maybe it wasn't Zach who made this ranch a success. Pearl probably pitched in, as well as the foreman, Charlie. There were undoubtedly more staff, those to keep the books, to order supplies, to do all the hundreds of things needed on a modern ranch.

It didn't surprise her that the animals looked healthy and fit. Or that the stable was meticulous. Most cowboys had a penchant for keeping things neat, at least when it came to the stock. From what she'd seen of her father, and most of the cowboys he ran with, the habit didn't extend to their homes. But then, Zach had Pearl, didn't he?

"We keep twenty horses here," Zach said, not bothering to turn his head to speak to her, just tossing the words over his shoulder. "There are two more barns and a corral on the east side of the ranch to hold the rest of the horses."

"How many head do you use in each string?" she asked.

He hesitated, but only for a second. She got the feeling he wasn't caught off guard by the question so much as the fact that she knew enough to ask it.

"Each man has ten head. Six circle horses, three cow horses and one night horse."

"That's more than I've seen work a herd."

"Up here in mountain country we cover a lot of ground each day. The horses work damn hard."

"I see," she said, trying to match his hurried gait. "So what kind of horse are you giving me?"

"I'm letting you ride Paladin," he said, slowing down in front of the second-to-the-last stall.

Taylor stopped beside him and looked at the horse she'd be riding for the next couple of days. He was a beauty. A mix of quarter horse and some big stock animal, maybe Percheron, from the looks of him. Large boned, blocky and clean limbed. Maybe sixteen hands. Not very much like the grade horses she'd grown up around. This one, Paladin, was dark bay, with one white stocking. She watched as Zach reached up slowly to touch his muzzle. The horse nickered and tossed his head.

"Shh, boy. Hush, now."

Zach's voice held the patience and tenderness a man might use to quiet his infant daughter or son. She recognized the tone. Not because it had been used on her, but because she'd listened to that tenderness all her life—around the horses.

She'd known men so tough they ate nails for breakfast and wood for lunch. But around their horses? Marshmallows. Pussycats.

"He seems a little spooky for a cow horse," she said, watching Paladin's eyes.

"He's good, if you know how to handle him." Zach turned to her, all the tenderness gone from his voice and his gaze. "If you can't ride, tell me now. Once we leave, we aren't coming back until the job's done."

She didn't even blink. "Where's his tack?"

"Right this way," Zach said.

She followed, studying him as he walked five paces in front of her. This view was the downfall of a lot of women. The back view. It was the jeans and how they molded to the rear end of a cowboy that did most of the damage. That and the broad shoulders. The combination was dangerous in even ordinary-looking men, but when they were part of a man as good-looking as Zach, it was lethal.

Good thing she wasn't taken in by such nonsense. A good behind did not a good mate make. She grinned. It was quite possible she'd just found her new motto. She'd stitch it on her couch pillow when she got home, just as a reminder.

Zach led her out the back of the stable, where she saw several smaller buildings clustered to her left. Two of them were mobile trailers, and the other three were made of wood. He headed for one of the wooden buildings, walking just fast enough for her to have to scramble.

He entered the one that said Tack Room on the door. She smelled the scent of leather, and once more, memories swamped her, bringing her back to the endless hours she'd spent caring for the rigs she and her family used. It wasn't glamorous work, but she'd liked it. It had been private time for her, when she'd let her imagination run free. Most of the time, she'd dreamed of being a rodeo star. Then again, she'd been a kid.

Zach walked over to a saddle sitting in one corner, nearly hidden beneath long bridle strands. "How's this suit you?" he asked.

"It looks like a fine saddle—" she watched his satisfied grin form "—if I were going to be riding a bronc in a rodeo."

His grin froze, then fell. She'd passed the pop quiz, much to his obvious annoyance.

Taking a quick glance around, past the saddle pads and blankets, the bridles, bits and the multitude of saddles, she spotted one that would work well for her. It was an Oregon-type saddle, with a high, full-sloped horn and a straight cantle. She went to it and checked the rigging straps, the latigo, the cinch and the stirrups. The workmanship looked fine, and as she ran a hand over the cantle, she could feel that it had been well taken care of.

"Bring her along, then," Zach said as he pulled down a pad and blanket. She reached for a bridle, bit, headstall, and then dallied a bit over her catch-all ropes.

She heard the impatient-sounding shuffle of Zach's boots on the wooden floor, but she wasn't going to rush her selection. He'd said something about working the bogs, and in her experience, pulling a six-hundred-pound steer out of thick, elastic mud required a rope that was sturdy and well made.

Finally, she made her decision. She wrapped the smaller equipment over her arm, then lifted the saddle. "I'm ready," she said, surprised to find Zach staring at her. The staring wasn't so bad; it was the object of his fascination that bothered her.

"Maybe if you let more women work on the ranch, you'd be used to seeing breasts by now," she said.

He jerked his head up, grunted, then turned and walked out the door. Taylor had a feeling she was going to pay for that comment later, but it had been worth it just to see the look on his face.

She hurried after him, keeping her grin to herself, just in case he looked back.

Of course, he didn't. He walked fast, straight to Paladin's stall, where he unceremoniously dumped the pad and blanket. He managed to avoid her gaze even then. "We ride in twenty minutes," he said gruffly. "I'm going to get the rest of the supplies."

She didn't take time to revel in her tiny victory. Instead, she put down the saddle and the other equipment, and walked slowly over to Paladin. She wanted him to get used to her before she fitted him out. Holding her hand out so he could get accustomed to her smell, she whispered to him in a singsong voice that was meant to soothe. "How do you put up with him?" she said, keeping her voice even and low. "Huh, boy? He's a big bully, isn't he? Hmm?"

"He sure as hell is."

Taylor froze. She didn't know where the voice had come from. Definitely not from the horse. "Hello?"

A boy stood up in the next stall. He was young—maybe twenty—and grinning broadly. She knew immediately that it was Cal, Frankie's fiancé. He was taller than Taylor had imagined, and much better looking. His dark hair crept over his collar, and his green eyes shone with intelligence.

"You're Taylor, aren't you?" he said.

"You got it. Hi, Cal."

"I'm real glad you decided to come," he said, moving over to the shoulder-height wall between them. He put his arms on the wood and smiled at her. "But I have to confess, I'm pretty nervous."

"Oh?"

"Well, Frankie puts a lot of stock in you. If you don't approve, then…"

"I can't promise anything, Cal."

"I know. But she also told me you were fair. And that you would have an open mind."

"Can I ask you something?"

"Sure," he said. "Anything you want."

"What was it about Frankie that made you pursue her?"

He took in a big breath of air, but his smile widened, too. "A lot of things. Her looks at first. She's so pretty…well, you know that. But she was so nice. Not just to me, but to everyone. The dining room at the hotel is real good, so me and the boys go there a lot. Especially in the summer. I'd stay after, and Frankie and I would talk and talk. I could say anything to her, you know? And she'd understand."

Taylor nodded. "Yes, I do know what you mean. Frankie is something special."

"Yes ma'am. And I mean to do right by her."

"I'm sure you do," she said, hoping against hope that by the time she left this ranch, she could convince Cal to find a new occupation. Not that a different job would change most of the cowboys she knew. They'd still be the same arrogant, chauvinistic jerks, even in a business suit. But Cal was still young, and frankly, she liked him. She didn't want to, but it was already too late for that. It didn't change her mind about seeing Frankie end up as a cowboy's wife, though. Especially one under the influence of Zach Baldwin. No matter how well intentioned and sweet Cal was, in the end it wouldn't matter.

Paladin nudged her hard, and she stumbled a bit.

"You need help?" Cal asked.

"No, thanks. But I'd better get my act in gear. Zach doesn't seem like a very patient man." She picked up the saddle blanket and turned to the horse.

"You really coming with us to drive the herd?" Cal asked.

She nodded.

"I'll be damned. I didn't think he'd ever let a woman ride. Not that I hold it against him or anything. He's got his reasons."

Taylor lifted the heavy saddle and put it on Paladin. The horse didn't seem to care much for that, so she petted his neck for a moment to calm him down. "Really?" she said over her shoulder. "And what reasons would those be?" She didn't want to spook the horse—or the boy. So she just kept petting the horse as she slowly moved to her right so she could see Cal. He was as handsome as Frankie had told her. His smile alone would make his passage through life an easy one, if he let it.

"He just says women and ranching don't mix," Cal said, his gaze moving between her and the horse.

"I have to agree with him there, but I'm curious as to why he thinks so."

Cal shrugged, then flashed that smile again. "Don't know. He's never told me in so many words. But some of the guys say…"

"Yes?"

Cal looked around, even walked to the edge of the stall so he could check the stable from one end to the other. Then he came into her stall and leaned against the wall. "Some of the guys say that a woman nearly stole the ranch out from under him. A woman he was gonna marry. Then there was a string of accidents here on the ranch. Bad accidents. Zach almost lost everything."

She cinched Paladin's saddle as she listened. She wasn't surprised to find that Zach had been engaged. It was obvious that he would attract a lot of women. But the fact that the woman he was engaged to almost stole his ranch was very interesting. She'd have to find out more about that story; it went a long way to explain his bitter attitude. "How long ago was this?" she asked Cal.

"Not sure. But it was before I got here, which was three years ago."

For a moment, she just concentrated on getting her horse ready to ride. Then she turned back to Cal, who'd been watching her carefully.

"You do that like a—"

"Cowboy?"

His grin broadened. "Yeah."

"Well, let me tell you a little secret, Cal," she said, turning so she could put her boot in the stirrup. "The horses don't care if you're a man or a woman. They just know strength and kindness.'' She led the horse out of the barn and swung herself up, settling on his back. Paladin wasn't happy about that, and it took all her concentration and strength to stay on him as he shifted around. Cal went for the reins, but Taylor waved him away.

She hadn't ridden an unwilling horse in years, but her training was ingrained. She held on tight, whispered soothing words, didn't let the horse rattle her. It worked, and Paladin settled, but she knew she'd have to really be on her toes with this one. *Thank you, Zach.*

She clicked her tongue, applied gentle pressure to Paladin's flanks, and they moved toward the big gate. ''It was good to meet you, Cal.''

''Nice meeting you, too,'' Cal said.

''We'll talk more. Lots more.''

''I'm gonna change your mind, Taylor. I swear I will.''

Taylor nodded, and although she didn't want to admit it, she almost hoped he was right.

ZACH WAS READY to ride. So where was she? Probably having it out with Paladin. The horse was a troublemaker, and even he'd had some difficulty saddling him before. Taylor was probably standing in the stall crying or something. Maybe she'd give it up now, and he'd be free of her.

No, she wasn't going to be that easy. She'd surprised him with her knowledge of saddles. He had to admit she knew something about rigging. But that didn't mean a whole lot. The real test was out *there*. On the range.

He was just about to go back to the barn when she appeared. She was walking Paladin. Walking him easy. Zach frowned. "You ready?"

She nodded. "All set."

"Then let's go," he said, turning his horse toward the mountains. He didn't look to see if she was following. He just knew she was.

There wasn't one thing about this situation that he liked. Not the woman, not the way she rode, not the way she looked. Nothing. He'd even had to take a lecture from Pearl on account of her. His aunt had made him promise to be nice to her. So okay, he wouldn't be mean. But he'd be tough. If Taylor wanted to ride with the big boys, then so be it.

He set out at a steady clip—just a fast walk, so the animals wouldn't get tired. They had a lot of territory to cover, and he wanted to get back before the sun went down. They'd need their energy.

Taylor came up beside him. He looked over to see how she'd equipped her mount, and had to grudgingly admit she'd done a good job.

Pearl had confirmed Taylor had been raised on a ranch. But she'd also told him that Taylor had been living in the city for years. She'd grown soft, sitting at her computer terminal. If he couldn't count on anything else, he could count on pain. If she hadn't ridden for five years, today's outing was going to hurt. Badly.

There wasn't any activity, any exercise that developed the muscles needed for riding. She'd be sore, all right. Sore enough, he hoped, to pack up and leave.

They rode in silence, which was the way he wanted it. Mile after mile, going from the flatland to the base of the mountain where there was the best chance of finding a bogged cow. Zach couldn't help but notice that whenever he took a swig of water from his canteen, so did Taylor. He felt a little foolish for bringing the second canteen. He'd been so sure she would finish hers way too soon.

"Are you going to ignore me the whole trip?" she asked finally.

He looked at her, still sitting comfortably in the saddle. Paladin, the traitor, was acting like a pussycat. But in a few more hours, Taylor wouldn't look so contented. Not if it were true that she hadn't ridden in years. "I'm not ignoring you."

"Then you won't mind if I ask you some questions?"

"Nope."

She moved closer to him, and though he was tempted to turn toward her, he just kept staring straight ahead.

"How'd you get the ranch?"

"My father left it to me."

"It's a lot of work, a ranch this size."

"That it is."

"You have a lot of people working for you?"

"Fifteen at the moment."

"And Pearl? Is she part of the staff, or does she have a stake?"

"Pearl's part owner."

Taylor didn't say anything for a long while, and he hoped that his curt responses had convinced her to stop asking questions. But somehow, he knew she wouldn't give up so easily.

"Zach?"

"Yeah?"

"Why are you a cowboy?" she asked.

He glanced at her, just to make sure she was serious. She was. "It's my job," he said.

"I know that. But why? Was it a choice, a dream from childhood? Or was it simply what was expected of you?"

He thought a moment. "All of those."

"You never thought of doing something else, then?"

"Nope."

"So you're happy?"

"I don't know. I guess."

"Well, if you're living out your dream, then it would seem to me that you'd be a very happy man."

"Who said I wasn't?"

"You said you 'guess.' That isn't a terribly strong statement."

"I don't think about happiness much. I just do what needs to be done."

"It's a hard life, here. I can guess that you don't take many vacations."

"When I need one, I take one."

"What about a wife?"

He looked at her again. She was studying him. He wished he'd never agreed to answer her questions. "What about it?"

"You don't have one."

"That's right."

"Why not?"

"What kind of a question is that?"

"A straightforward one. Why aren't you married?"

"That's none of your business."

"I'd like the article to be fair," she said. "Unbiased."

"Is that a threat?"

"No," she said. "Not at all. I just want to make sure I understand. Isn't it traditional for a rancher to have a wife and family?"

"Traditional? I don't know what that means." Zach waited. All he heard was Taylor muttering under her breath. But there was another sound, too.

"You know—husband, wife, baby in the—"

"Quiet," he said, pulling up on Falcon.

"I will not. It's my job to ask questions—"

"Will you shut up?" He glared at her. "I'm trying to hear."

She flushed a bit, looked away, but at least she was silent. Zach jerked his attention away from the woman and listened as hard as he could. A minute went by. Then two. Just when he'd figured he'd made a mistake, he heard it again.

"I heard that," Taylor said. She pointed east. "It was coming from there."

He shook his head. "Quiet now. You can't tell so easily, not here. There are too many echoes."

She stilled again, and he watched her as he tried to locate the bawling cow. Once again he heard the sorrowful sound, and this time he knew where it was coming from. East, dammit.

He urged Falcon on, and then he made the mistake of looking at Taylor. Her satisfied smile made him angry all over again. Good thing he was going to do some real work now. He'd sweat the vinegar out of himself.

THE COW WASN'T mired too badly. Taylor imagined that she was more scared and tired than anything else. It wasn't hard to see how she'd gotten trapped. There was a waterfall about fifty feet away, with a nice pond underneath. Several wet patches made mostly of mud and rock surrounded the pond. The cow had been thirsty, and had tried to get at the fresh water. Only the mud hadn't let her go.

"Well?" Zach said, sitting with his hands folded over his saddle horn.

"Well what?"

"You said you'd ranched. Now's your chance to prove it."

"So it's like that, is it?"

"Hey, I don't know you from Adam. How am I

supposed to let you ride herd if I don't know that you know your stuff?''

"I believe it would be more accurate to say that you don't know me from *Eve*."

He smiled, but it wasn't a friendly smile.

Taylor assessed the situation before her. She was on a strange and somewhat spooky horse who'd been testing her all day, waiting for her to relax, get sloppy— but she'd been vigilant. And she was paying for that in spades. She hadn't ridden in years, and already her muscles were complaining. By tonight, she was going to be sorry she'd ever seen this horse. But right now, she couldn't think about that. She had a job to do.

The cow must weigh around six hundred pounds, and it looked like John Wayne over there didn't intend to help. As far as she could tell, there was nothing to do but get the job done.

She moved Paladin a little closer—which he didn't care for—pressing him hard with her thighs, and holding him close to the bit. Then she got her rope out, and started swinging it in a gentle circle. She gauged the distance, the wind, the angle of the cow's head. When she was ready, and not a second before, she let fly.

It fell short.

Cursing silently, she pulled it back and began the ritual once more. This time, she hit pay dirt.

Now came the really tricky part: getting Paladin to cooperate. She eased out the slack in the rope, and pulled back on the horse's reins. Slowly, she urged the horse backwards, cooing softly to him the whole time.

At first all the horse did was try to get away. But she hadn't gotten so soft that she didn't know how to stop that. When Paladin eventually realized they weren't going anywhere else, he started backing up.

The cow started bawling again, sounding as though she were being killed instead of saved. But Taylor didn't pay her any attention. She concentrated on the horse, and the rope. Finally the cow moved, but not much. Just about a foot. At this rate, the cow would starve to death before Taylor could get her free.

Back where she came from, they would never expect a single cowhand to do this job. They'd bring a tractor up to the bog, or at the very least a team of hands.

She looked over at Zach. He was studying the situation, his brow creased and his attention fixed on the end of her rope. Taylor wouldn't quit. Not for anything. She moved the cow another foot, her arm and thigh muscles quivering with the strain.

Then she saw another rope fly over the cow's head. So he'd decided to help after all.

His horse came up beside Paladin, and then the cow started to really move out of the bog. It wasn't exactly a pretty operation, but it was working. After another half hour or so—a half hour during which her body was tested to the limit—the cow's front legs reached firm earth. Taylor didn't let up, not until she saw all four legs out of the mud. Then she relaxed. She looked over at Zach. They stared at each other for a long moment. Neither one of them blinked. He was the one who moved first.

He got down out of his saddle to retrieve their ropes from the cow's neck. Only the cow wasn't in a very cooperative mood.

First it darted at Paladin, who reared up so quickly that Taylor barely held on. Then it darted at Falcon, who shifted suddenly to the right. The horse's flank hit Zach square in the back. Hard.

As if in slow motion, Zach's arms went out to his sides, his eyes widened, the beginning of a shout formed…and then he began his descent. A perfect arc. He landed face down in the bog.

Taylor was too stunned to move. She just watched him lie there, as if he were making a snow angel in the mud. He even sank a little. She was just climbing down off Paladin when he finally moved, lifting his head up to spit.

She couldn't help laughing. She tried, but it was no good. Especially when she saw Falcon and the cow, happily chewing on some fresh green grass as if they'd been friends for life.

Zach's curse echoed all over the mountain.

Chapter Four

Zach spit out a mouthful of mud, then pulled himself to his feet. He heard Taylor's laughter, and her attempt to stifle it, which made him even angrier than if she'd just let it out and gotten it over with. His eyes stung, and he went to wipe them, but his hands were so muddy that it would only make things worse. Dammit to hell and back.

"I'm sorry," she said. "I know I shouldn't laugh. It's really not funny."

He looked in her direction, but he couldn't see her well with all the gunk in his eyes. "Right," he said, his voice gruff with the words he wanted to say still stuck in his throat. "Make sure the animals stay clear of the bog," he said as he started toward the pond at the base of the waterfall.

"Okay, boss."

Each step was about as uncomfortable as it could be. Mud had gotten under his shirt, in his pants, in his hair. It was all her fault. He never should have let her come. He should have chased her off his ranch the moment he'd seen her.

He stepped over some shrubs and rocks, and finally arrived at the water hole. Still muttering curses that would make Charlie blush, he started to unbutton his shirt. It wasn't until it was half off him that he realized he couldn't just strip and clean himself off properly. Not with *her* standing twenty feet away.

He could tell her not to look. But she would. Hell, if the roles were reversed and it was her getting naked, *he'd* look. So what if she did? It wasn't like a woman her age hadn't seen a naked man before.

The only thing was, the water was spring runoff from the winter snow. It was mighty cold—cold enough to make a man's body shrink up to nothing. It shouldn't matter, but it did. Bad enough that she'd see him in the altogether. He didn't want her seeing him after he'd come out of the icy water.

But he couldn't stay the way he was. There was only one thing to do. He sat down, pulled off his boots and his socks, took his wallet out of his jeans pocket, then stood up again. Without looking back at her, but knowing she was watching, he started walking.

He almost stopped when his feet hit the water. It was like ice—so cold it burned. Gritting his teeth, he went right in, not stopping, even though he knew he was going to have to ride all the way back to the ranch in wet clothes. He was up to his waist in water when he realized he hadn't brought his blanket. It didn't matter. He was going to freeze to death anyway. That would show Pearl. Making him bring a woman along was just plain bad luck.

Accidents had happened too many times for him not to believe it, even though Pearl told him it was nonsense. Five different times. Five different women. Someone getting hurt each time. And now, Taylor. Number six.

Swallowing hard, unable to keep his teeth from chattering, he brought his hands up to clean his face. He managed two splashes, then he turned around to go back.

Taylor was standing at the water's edge, holding a blanket for him. He tried to stop shaking, but it was no use. The cold had gone deep. All the way to his core.

"That water must be freezing," she said.

He couldn't speak, which was probably a good thing. What he wanted to say to her wasn't very gentlemanly. He just lugged himself out of the water.

She held the blanket out to him, and he reached for it, but then she pulled it back.

"Hey!"

"Take off your clothes," she said.

"What?"

"Go ahead. You'll just get the blanket wet, and you'll never get warm."

"Just give me the damn blanket," he said, his voice shivering along with the rest of him.

"Don't be a fool, Zach. You can't ride all the way back to the ranch like that. You'll catch pneumonia.

Look at your hands, for heaven's sake. They're turning blue already.''

He looked down. She was right. He had to get warm. "Close your eyes," he said.

"What?"

"You heard me."

She sighed. "All right. Just hurry."

He waited until she'd done as he asked, then he went to work on his buttons. Only he couldn't work them. He had no feeling in his fingers. He kept trying, but got nowhere. Then he tried the buttons on his jeans. Again, no luck. He swore loudly.

"Well?" she asked.

"I can't get them open," he said. "So just give me the damn blanket."

She opened her eyes. He expected her to laugh, but she didn't. Matter of fact, she looked downright concerned. She put the blanket on the rock next to her, then she came toward him.

"What are you doing?" he asked, his voice shaking.

"I'm getting you out of those clothes."

He stepped back. "No you're not."

"I am," she said. "I'm not going to let you freeze to death. What would I tell Pearl?"

She reached him, standing so close that he could see the tiny flecks of gold in her deep brown eyes. She finished unbuttoning his shirt, but he couldn't feel her. What surprised him was that he *wanted* to feel her. It was probably some primal thing. The last crazy wishes of a dying man.

Then she started on his jeans. He couldn't believe she was undressing him like this. No woman had ever taken off his jeans, unless she were going to take off her own, right quick. But he was too cold to be embarrassed. Well, maybe not. As she got to the last button, he finally felt something. Her hand.

Not that his body was in any condition to respond. Nope, he was still shriveled up like a raisin. She started to pull his pants down, and he jerked away. "I can do the rest," he said.

She had the decency to back off. "Do it fast."

She turned around to get the blanket; he struggled to get his shirt off as fast as he could. But his wrists got in the way, and he couldn't unbutton the damn cuffs. Of all the days not to have worn a western shirt with snaps.

"Let me," she said, her voice strangely soft. "Can you hold this?"

She had the blanket spread out in her hands. He took the ends, shielding most of his body from her view. Then she unbuttoned each of his cuffs, and took back the blanket. She kept it steady, about chest high.

"Go on," she said. "Turn around. Get those clothes off."

He obeyed. He shook off his shirt, then concentrated on his pants. He was acutely aware that she was so near. That she was watching his every move. That soon he'd be bare-assed naked in front of her.

He felt like a fool for caring. It wasn't like him at all. He wasn't shy, not in the least. It was *her*. She was making him crazy, making him feel like one of his boys. *Oh, hell.* He shoved his pants down, and started to turn and face the music, when he felt the blanket on his shoulders. Then her arms were around him, and he was cocooned in her embrace, the blanket covering him up from shoulder to calf.

"Hold this," she said. He did. Then she started rubbing him, very briskly, on his back, his arms. He still shivered like crazy, but at least he felt her hands now. She moved in front of him and rubbed his chest, her face a study in concentration. It was hard to be mad at her when she worked so fiercely to warm him up. He tried harder.

She moved around in back of him again, and he felt her hands on his behind.

"Hey!"

"Get over it," she said.

He gritted his teeth once more, and waited impatiently for her to move down to his legs. It was a long wait. Long enough for her ministrations to have a side effect. He felt the front of him warming up...

He jerked away from her. "I'm good. I'm fine. Thank you."

"But—"

"I said, I'm fine."

She crossed her arms and looked at him. He'd seen that look before, on most of the women he'd known. Exasperation. He didn't care. He just reached down and picked up his shirt and pants. The idea of putting his pants on again held no appeal, but he wasn't going to ride buck naked.

"Come with me," she said, turning to walk back to the horses. "I've got something you can put on."

He looked at his pants, dripping wet, freezing cold. And then he went after her.

TAYLOR HAD NEVER been happier to see a ranch. Her muscles, particularly the *gluteus maximus,* screamed in pain. Her thighs were killing her, even her back hurt. The whole ride home, she kept thinking about that hot tub she'd seen on the deck, imagining the moment she could sink down in the steaming water. When that thought hadn't been enough to keep her mind from her aches and pains, she'd looked over at Zach. It was tempting to feel sorry for him. He truly looked as though he were the most miserable man on the planet. But then she thought about how he blamed her for his misfortune, and the temptation vanished like magic.

She'd been far too nice to him as it was. He wasn't exactly subtle about the fact that he didn't want her on his precious ranch. He hadn't even been gracious enough to admit that she was a good rider, and a very capable cowhand. Oh, no. That would be admitting he was mistaken, and that was something a cowboy would never do.

Whatever misery he was in, he deserved. Stubborn mule. But she'd have her revenge. In just a few more minutes.

The horses, particularly Falcon, picked up speed after they passed the first corral. Soon, the fast walk became a canter, with both animals determined to get back to their nice, safe stalls.

Taylor looked around, anxious to see who was around the barn, who would actually see their arrival. Good, Charlie was there. And about six other men, none of whom she'd seen before. One was older, and the rest looked to be around Cal's age. She grinned. This was going to be delicious.

Glancing over at Zach, she saw him try to rein in Falcon, but the horse, bless him, would have none of it. He wanted to go home. There was no way Zach was going to get out of his little predicament.

As miserable as he'd looked on the way in, it wasn't half as wretched as he looked when he got a load of his buddies. It was all Taylor could do not to laugh out loud.

Falcon reached the barn first, and she urged Paladin on, not wanting to miss a moment. She got there just as she heard Charlie say, "What the hell...?"

"Shut up, Charlie," Zach said, sounding more like a grizzly than a man.

"What's that you got on?"

"I said, shut up."

"But—"

Zach held up his hand. He climbed off Falcon with all the dignity he could muster—considering the fact that he was wearing her very stretched-out pink-knit stirrup pants with matching V-neck sweater.

He glared at the men around him. "First one who laughs gets to muck out the stables for the next year."

No one spoke. But had they been cartoons, their eyes would have *boinged* out about two feet.

Funny how she hardly felt any pain as she dismounted to lead Paladin to his stall. And gosh, wasn't it something, how her laughter echoed off the walls of the barn?

TAYLOR CREPT OUT to the hot tub just as the sun dipped behind the mountains. She blessed whoever had invented hot tubs, and praised the wisdom of whoever had decided to install this one on the ranch. The steam wafted over the big wooden tub, making the deck seem otherworldly. Maybe like heaven.

She put her towel down quickly, then climbed the two steps to the tub itself. With a sigh that came all the way from her toes, she eased into the hot water. Closing her eyes, she sank down until she was sitting, the water all the way up to her neck. Nothing had ever felt so good.

For a long time, she stayed perfectly still. Until she could honestly say that she was warmed to the core. It was so quiet, so peaceful, she almost wished that she didn't hate ranch life so much.

Sighing again, she let her thoughts go. No more worrying about the article, or Frankie, or cowboys, or anything troubling. Not while she was this close to bliss.

She pictured the waterfall from this afternoon. She'd

been so busy with the cow, and then Zach, that she hadn't really taken the time to appreciate the beauty of her surroundings. She wasn't used to the mountains: the lush greens, the tall trees. Growing up, she'd been in desert country, with its own kind of beauty. In Houston, she saw some trees, but mostly she saw tall buildings and shopping malls, traffic and supermarkets...

No, she wasn't going to think of anything unpleasant. She slid her mind back to the waterfall. To the pond. To Zach.

She'd never admit it to anyone, but the truth was, when he got naked, she'd peeked. Which was stupid, because now she knew for a fact that his body was perfect. At least from the back view. Not that she was crazy about naked men. Unless she cared about a guy, she'd just as soon not see him in his birthday suit. But for Zach, she'd made an exception.

On purely aesthetic grounds, of course.

Looking at his back, even when he was shivering like that, had been like looking at the statue of David. Zach's body was perfectly sculpted. Not too muscled, not too hairy. And rubbing him the way she had— feeling all those muscles—*whoa!* Especially the *gluteus maximus.* Now that wasn't fair at all. She'd kill to have a firm butt like his.

It was a pity that such a great-looking man had the soul of a cowboy. Why couldn't he have been a pilot, or a detective, or even a CPA? But no. In yet another illustration that God had a wicked sense of humor, the handsomest man she'd ever seen was not just a cowboy, but a card-carrying, die-with-his-boots-on rancher.

She shifted a bit on her seat, sinking down an inch lower. If she could have breathed under water, she would have gone deeper, it felt so good.

"You fall asleep like that, you're going to drown."

Taylor's eyes snapped open, and she saw Zach standing on the deck on the other side of the hot tub. He was shirtless, and for a wild second she thought he might be completely naked. She sat up, so she could see better.

When she realized what she had done, she looked down immediately, more to shield her own embarrassment than to give Zach any privacy. But of course, he wasn't naked. He wore swimming trunks, just as she wore her bathing suit. It was her own imagination run amok, a direct result of too much testosterone in the air. Cowboys! She always got in trouble around cowboys.

Zach was now easing himself into the water, his arm muscles corded with tension as he lowered his body.

Again, she jerked her gaze away. She had to stop thinking like that. What was going on with her? She wasn't the type to go gaga over a man's physique. She'd seen plenty of babes in her time, and not one of them had made her lose her cool.

Until Zach.

"Oh, man. I thought I'd never be warm again," he said.

His camaraderie surprised her. After what had happened at the barn, she'd felt sure he'd never speak to her again in any tone, let alone in this rather casual, somewhat intimate whisper.

"I know. Today was pretty rough," she said, trying to match his demeanor. "That water was freezing."

"I imagine you're pretty sore," he said, looking at her mildly.

"I'm okay."

"We covered a lot of territory."

"Oh, I'm feeling it. But don't worry. I'll be fine by the time we head out to take the herd."

He looked at her for a long while, then closed his eyes. She wasn't sure what to do. This friendliness confused her. She didn't trust it. On the other hand, maybe she'd actually proved herself to him today, and now that nonsense of not taking a woman on the drive was over.

"Can I ask you a question?"

He opened one eye, nodded, then closed it again.

"What's with the boys' club?"

"It's a long story," he said. "My priorities on this ranch are to take care of business, and to help the kids out. Women are a distraction."

She studied him for a while, watching the water curl up to his chest, matting his dark hair. "Pardon my frankness, but what a crock."

He laughed, making her jump a little.

"That wasn't meant to be funny."

"I know. It's just that not too many people are quite that frank with me."

"Why not?"

He shrugged lazily. "I'm not sure. About the only two people who knock heads with me are Charlie and Pearl."

"A good reason for hiring boys instead of men, eh?"

The right side of his mouth curled up into a half-baked smile. "Hadn't thought of it that way myself, but now that you mention it, I think you're right."

"And that doesn't embarrass you?"

"Not in the least. This ranch isn't a democracy. It's a dictatorship."

"With you as czar."

"That's right."

"So you don't mind at all that you're completely reactionary, and that the boys that work for you see you as someone to emulate?"

"The boys are smart enough to understand what's good for them."

"And women aren't good for them?"

"They can be. But only when the boys are mature enough to deal with them." He sat up a little, and this time he looked at her with both eyes. "Ms. Reed, the boys that come here are troubled. They've messed up a few too many times. They come here for a second chance. Maybe a last chance. This ranch is about hard work, and responsibility. Not about dances and flirting and all that other garbage that comes with that territory.''

"But don't you see? That's where boys need the most training—with women. They need to learn to respect women. To understand the differences, and the similarities.''

"No boy from this ranch will ever disrespect a lady. Not while they're on my land.''

"And what about when they leave? Do you think you've taught them anything but that women are dangerous?''

"No. You're forgetting that they see Pearl every day.''

"Yes, but that's not quite the same. From what I gather, it's girls their own age...or yours...that you're teaching them to fear.''

"I've taught them to respect themselves and others, if I'm successful—which I'm not all the time. But mostly, what I do here works.''

"I can see you believe that. And I'm not denying that what you're doing is good, and needed. I just don't see that telling the boys that women are bad luck is doing them any favors.''

She scooted a little toward him, aware that he hadn't shifted his gaze at all. He was really studying her. But now was no time to be shy. "I had a friend at college,'' she said. "Her parents were into healthful living. They were strict vegetarians, and made sure their children were, too. No white sugar. No bleached flour. They even made sure the kids didn't have sweets at school or with friends. Know what my friend did when she went to college?''

''Ate every piece of junk food in sight?''

''Bingo.''

He crossed his arms over his chest. ''So you think that the minute the boys leave here, they're going to go crazy, huh?''

''I wouldn't be surprised.''

''I would. You don't have to believe me. But I've followed the boys who've left here. They may not all be Sunday school teachers, but they're good men. And those that have kids are good fathers. Besides, Pearl is here. She doesn't let them forget that she's a lady.''

''I see,'' she said. ''Well, it's your playground. I guess you get to make the rules.''

''That's right. I do.''

He leaned his head back once more. She could have continued the argument, but there was no point. He wasn't going to change in an hour, or two weeks. But she had a suspicion that his rules were based on something other than the ''distraction'' principle. Something told her the no-women rule was more for his protection than any of the boys.

Suddenly, she was tired. Bone weary. She didn't care about dinner. All she wanted was bed. After one last look at Zach, she turned and began her climb out of the hot tub.

''Taylor.''

She grabbed her towel and wrapped it around her body. ''Yes?''

"I'm going out tomorrow to check on the high pasture. I need to do some repairs to the corrals and the traps."

"Okay."

"You're coming with me."

"I am?"

"Pack for three days."

"But—"

He stood up. "You want to ride with us on the drive?"

She nodded.

"Then you come with me tomorrow."

"But—"

"It's my playground, remember?"

She closed her mouth and turned to leave, her good mood completely gone. The stubborn son-of-a—

"Taylor."

She whirled on him. "What?"

"You're gonna need this." He tossed something at her, and she dropped her towel in order to catch it. It was a tube of liniment.

When she looked up at him again, his gaze had moved from her face to her body. Although her swimsuit was modest, it was still a swimsuit. She grabbed her towel quickly and wrapped it around her once more.

"What time are we leaving in the morning?" she asked.

"Be at breakfast at five. We leave at six. Sharp."

Chapter Five

"One has to wonder why you're taking her with you. Could it be that you like her company?"

Zach glared at Pearl, even though he knew she wasn't fazed by his temper. "I'm taking her with me to keep her away from the others," he said, walking to the coffeepot.

"You amaze me, Zachary. What do you think she'll do to the boys? Cast a spell? She's a nice woman. A journalist. She's not out here to snag herself a seventeen-year-old."

Zach poured himself a mug of the strong coffee, then filled up two thermoses. "Do you know how she takes her coffee?" he asked.

"Why don't you ask her?"

He grunted, positive that she took it with artificial sugar and probably flavored cream. Well, not today. Today she was going to have coffee like a real cowhand's. Black and strong.

Pearl turned back to the big frying pan where she

was scrambling three dozen eggs. But he saw her shaking her head.

"Pearl, I know what I'm doing. I'm just being cautious. The drive is in a few days. The last thing we need is to have half the boys in the hospital."

Pearl laughed. "What power you think women have! And what weak constitutions you assign to your boys."

"That's right. Exactly right. When it comes to sex, women do have power. Men become helpless fools."

She looked at him seriously. "Not all men, Zach."

"You're right. But by the time you find out who the fools are, it's too late."

"The only fool I see is the one pouring the coffee."

"You know as well as I do that every time a woman has come onto this ranch, something's gone wrong. The accident, the robbery. The time Joe Allen got hurt. Face it, women and this ranch don't mix."

"Well, thank you very much."

"You know I don't mean you."

"So there are exceptions?"

"Only one."

"Zach, just because it hasn't worked out before doesn't mean it's never going to work out. It's not healthy for a man like you to be without a woman."

"I'm not without women."

"I said 'a woman.' Singular. Someone special."

"That's the last thing I need."

"Can't you even entertain the idea that things can change? That all women aren't bad luck?"

"There's too much evidence for me to disregard it, Pearl, and you know that. It's not like I haven't tried."

"You haven't tried in over five years."

"That's because I learned from my mistakes. You know, it occurs to me that no one, including you, darlin', gave a hoot about my bachelorhood until yesterday. Why don't we just go back to the way it should be, okay? You know, everyone minding their own business."

"You *are* my business. But I'll let it go. For now." She shook her head sadly. "Are you finished packing?"

"No, I still have some things to do."

"Then go on. Get out of here. Breakfast will be ready in about fifteen minutes."

He got his mug, but before he left he went to Pearl's side and slipped her a kiss on the cheek.

"What was that for?" she said, smiling.

He smiled back at her. "'Cause I like the way you make coffee."

Her laughter followed him to the door.

"Zach?"

He stopped, turned. "Yeah?"

"Don't you think Frankie is an exception, too?"

He'd gotten to know Taylor's sister over the course of the summer, and he also had seen how Cal had taken to her. She was a nice girl. And as long as she stayed in town, he wished her and Cal all the best. "Maybe," he said.

"Tell that to Taylor, okay? It's important."

He nodded, then headed for his room. He knew Pearl didn't understand his feelings about having women here on the ranch, and he wished things had been different. Having Taylor here reminded him of things he didn't like to think about. Like the way she smelled like flowers and honey. But she also made him remember how he'd made such a fool of himself over Belinda. He'd fallen for her, believed her when she'd said she'd loved him. And then she'd left him for a cattle broker, but not before she'd nearly wiped out his bank account.

And she wasn't the worst. At least with Belinda, he was the one to pay the price. When his bad luck started rubbing off on the boys, it was time to make some hard and fast rules. There was one thing Pearl couldn't deny: since he'd made the rule about no women on the ranch, no one had gotten hurt. That was evidence enough for him.

Zach climbed the stairs and walked slowly to his room. He passed Taylor's door, and wondered if he should check on her. Make sure she hadn't overslept. No. From what he knew about Taylor, she wasn't the type to miss out on a thing. She'd be up and ready to go. Probably in the shower about now.

A quick flash of her from last night, when her towel had fallen, made him slow his steps. Could he risk taking her on the drive? What if nothing had changed? What if something happened to the boys? He'd never be able to forgive himself.

Yesterday's ride hadn't convinced her to give up on

the idea of going on the drive. But the next couple of days would. He'd see to it.

BY THE TIME he got finished packing and came back downstairs, the table was already set, and the juice and milk had been set on the sideboard. He went toward the kitchen, but just before he reached the door he heard Taylor's voice. He slowed his pace, straining to hear.

"Where do you want these?" she asked.

"Just put them on that table," Pearl said. "So what did you do?"

"There wasn't much I could do. I left the ranch. Got a job in Houston."

"Did you ever see him again?"

Zach took a step closer to the door.

"Yes, several times. He ended up with a barrel racer from Montana."

"I think it's a crying shame. Did he ever tell you why he wanted to call off the wedding?"

"He didn't have to. He wanted to do the rodeo circuit and work as an extra hand on the local ranches. I wanted to settle down and have a family, which meant he would have had to get a real job. The rodeo won."

Zach didn't hear anything for a moment, and he wondered if Pearl or Taylor were coming to the dining room. He should announce himself, but he decided to wait a little longer. Some things about Taylor were falling into place.

"I'm sorry, honey," Pearl said. "But they're not all like him."

"Maybe not. But I sure have met my share."

"You and Zach are more alike than you know," Pearl said.

"How do you mean?" Taylor asked.

"You're both convinced that women and ranching don't mix."

"Now wait a minute," Taylor said. "I never said that. I think ranching and women mix fine. It's women and cowboys who don't."

"Now, just because you had one bad—"

"One? No. It wasn't just one. It was every. From my father, to the neighbors, to Ben. They were all alike. All members of an exclusive club that I wasn't allowed to join. The irony of it is that my sisters never minded. Neither of them particularly wanted to work on the ranch."

"But you did?"

"Yes. I did. Until I was fifteen, there was nothing I wanted more than to be a cowgirl."

"What happened at fifteen?"

"I won a chance to go on the rodeo circuit, but my father wouldn't let me go."

"Why?"

"Because I was a girl. He said he'd have let me go if I were a boy, but no daughter of his was gonna do the circuit."

"Maybe he thought it was dangerous for you."

"I doubt it. He just thought I'd be better off spending my summer learning to cook and sew. Learning to be a rancher's wife instead of a rancher.''

"Some women are very happy being ranchers' wives.''

"True, but only because they're willing to compromise.''

"But we all have to compromise in one way or another. That's just life.''

"Some compromises are too big," Taylor said. "At the very least, a woman should know what she's in for. That life with a cowboy is no picnic. And all I want to do now is tell the truth.''

"I'm sorry it was so rough for you," Pearl said.

"Don't be. I'm happy now. I've got the life I want.''

"Well, I'm glad that you've found your place in life," Pearl said. "Now how about you find a place for those potatoes?''

Zach got moving. He coughed a little, just to announce his presence, then he went into the kitchen. Taylor had the platter of hash browns in her hands, and Pearl stood over a frying pan full of bacon.

"Morning," Taylor said.

"Morning," he replied, trying not to notice how the pair of jeans she had on hugged her curves. Trying not to think about what she'd looked like in that bathing suit.

What he did need to think about was what he'd just heard. She'd been hurt by her father, and she'd been left at the altar by a cowboy. But was she going to do something about that? Take it out on him, or his boys?

The next few days would tell him. He'd watch her like a hawk. Find out what she was really going to write. What she was going to tell her sister. Suddenly, he felt sorry for Cal. There was no way Taylor was going to give him her blessing. Not with that attitude.

"If you can manage to take your eyes off our guest's backside," Pearl whispered in his ear, "you can take the eggs into the other room."

He looked away, mad at himself and at Pearl. His aunt didn't miss a thing. "I was just making sure she didn't trip."

"Oh, sure," she said. "I'm packing enough food for three days. Is that right?"

He walked over to the big platter of steaming scrambled eggs and lifted it by the sides. "That's right. We'll probably be back in two days, but you never know. The traps might be in a lot worse shape than I think."

"It's still awfully cold, so I hope you'll be good enough to check Taylor's kit."

"Pearl, I may be a jerk, but I'm not cruel. I'll make sure she has everything she needs."

"I'm sure you will, honey. Now go on. The boys are gonna be here in a moment."

He headed for the dining room. Several of the men—including Charlie, Big Danny and Jesse—were already seated. But instead of taking their normal places, they had all gathered around Taylor. Typical.

He put the platter down, and moved over to where

Jesse was sitting, right next to Taylor. "Did you forget something?" he said.

The boy looked up at him, then his face got all flushed. "Sorry," he said, standing so quickly that the chair almost fell. "I didn't mean to take your seat."

"Okay, then," Zach said, scowling. "Before you sit down, go out and make sure everyone is up and heading this way."

"They are, boss."

"I said—"

"Okay, okay," Jesse said, backing away. "I'll go check."

Zach watched the boy hurry out, then he took his seat. Everyone got quiet, and Zach knew it was because of him. But he didn't give a damn. Nothing about this week had gone particularly right, and he wasn't looking forward to the next three days, either. But at least he'd be keeping *her* away from the ranch.

But he had no illusions that his trip to the high pasture was going to be easy. Just sitting next to Taylor made him uncomfortably aware of her. Even though he knew that she wasn't his type—that she was, in fact, a woman with a score to settle—he still found himself attracted to her.

She touched his shoulder, and he jerked his head in her direction. All she was doing was passing the eggs, but she didn't move her hand. It stayed on his shoulder, light, yet the warmth of her seemed to seep right through the material.

Meeting her gaze made him remember her hands on his back and on his chest, rubbing through the blanket.

She smiled, then her gaze shifted to the platter. He took it from her, and she moved her hand. He let out the breath he'd been holding. It was going to be a very long few days, and an even longer few nights.

TAYLOR HOPED like crazy that she hadn't forgotten anything. The last thing she wanted to do was to ask Zach for help. He'd been surly as a bear all morning, and it didn't take a genius to figure out that his mood was because of her.

The rational part of her understood that he was just upset because a female had the audacity to invade his male bastion, but she still couldn't stop some very old feelings from bubbling to the surface. There had only been two men in her life that she'd really loved. Her father and Ben. Both of them had made it very clear that they loved the ranch life more than they loved her.

Now she was faced with yet another man who didn't want her around. The only thing that kept her going was the fact that this time, she was going to get even. This time, she was going to tell the world the truth, and once she'd done that, she just knew her old hurts would finally be healed.

She'd started the article last night, and before she'd gone to bed she'd written three pages. Three scathing pages. She smiled.

"You ready?" Zach asked as he mounted Falcon.

"Yep."

"You didn't forget anything? Any girl things? There aren't any drugstores where we're going."

"I didn't forget anything."

He shifted on his saddle, then spurred Falcon to a walk, heading back out the same way they'd gone yesterday. Taylor clicked her tongue, and Paladin followed Falcon.

She wondered what was in store for her. She'd learned from Charlie that they'd be making sure the high pasture corral was ready for the herd, and checking out the cattle traps—the wooden gates the men would drive the herd through so that the cows could be vaccinated, counted, and the young animals branded. It was going to be rough work, and she was so sore already that the thought of what was in front of her should have been upsetting. Only, it wasn't.

Along with old bitter memories, another fire had been stoked this morning. Despite her soreness, despite the fact that she really wasn't wanted on this trip, she was excited. The country they would cross was so beautiful it made her ache inside. The work was hard, but it was also satisfying. Immediate. Better than any aerobics class at her gym. She'd always liked the physical part of being a cowhand, although she rarely admitted it.

The sense of anticipation helped her put her old wounds back in the recesses of her mind where they belonged. The liniment Zach had given her last night helped her to ride with a modicum of comfort. Zach or no Zach, she was going to enjoy this. And she was going to prove that, even though she didn't have a penis, she was still a fine cowhand.

TAYLOR WANTED OFF. She'd been sore enough this morning, but now, after riding for a good four hours, she was in acute misery. No matter how she shifted on her saddle, she couldn't get comfortable. The only thing she could think to do was stop, put on some more liniment, take two aspirins, and pray the combination would help.

"Zach."

He turned to look at her, and she realized that it was the first time they'd made eye contact, or even spoken, since leaving the ranch.

"I need to take a break," she said.

He frowned, but he pulled up on his reins. "Go on ahead," he said.

"Thanks." She stopped Paladin, then gingerly dismounted, reaching into her saddlebag for the liniment and the aspirin. She also took out her roll of toilet paper, just to make sure Zach didn't think she was stopping because she was hurting so badly. If he suspected, she knew he would use the information against her. He'd complain that she was only a weak woman, and that if she was sore now, she couldn't possibly go on the drive.

She hurried toward a thick patch of trees and ducked out of sight. She unzipped her pants and pulled them down, keeping an eye out for Zach. Then she started to apply the liniment, wincing from her own touch.

It took a few moments, but finally she finished, and she pulled up her pants. Now for the aspirin. Damn. She'd forgotten her canteen. Oh, well. She'd take them later. She closed her hand around the pills and walked back to the clearing. Just as she left the tree cover, she saw Zach. He stood in front of Paladin, holding her canteen out to her.

"You forgot your water," Zach said.

So he'd guessed her secret. She wondered if he also knew about the liniment.

"Go on, take it," he said.

"How did you... Were you watching me?"

"No. I wasn't watching you," he said gruffly. "Just take the canteen so we can get going."

She did, but grudgingly. She didn't believe him. Maybe he was trying to pay her back for looking at his bottom yesterday. Blushing furiously, she drank down a good deal of water, then recapped the canteen.

He walked back to Falcon, put his foot in the stirrup, and hoisted himself onto the horse's back. "We have another hour of riding till we get to the pasture. Are you going to be able to make it?"

She looked at him for a long while. His handsome features were set in stone. He didn't look at her at all— just stared straight ahead, neither frowning nor smiling.

Was it possible he was giving her an out because he was concerned about her? That he was just thinking of her comfort? No. Not him. Not with his agenda.

She went over to Paladin, and climbed up into the

saddle, a hiss of pain escaping, despite herself. "I'll be fine, thanks," she said.

"It won't hurt you to take an extra aspirin," he said, his voice low and tinged with impatience. "But don't take more than three. If it's real bad, tell me, and we'll stop." Then he clicked his tongue at Falcon, and rode off ahead of her.

She didn't move for a bit. She didn't like this new development. It was easier for her to think of Zach as a louse, pure and simple. First, finding out about the kind of boys he chose to hire had chipped away at her determination to dislike him, and now this. If she wasn't careful, she'd start thinking that there was more to this cowboy than just surly obstinacy.

She urged Paladin forward, barely feeling the effects of the liniment. She was grateful that she and the horse had come to something of an understanding. If she'd had to fight him the way she had yesterday, she'd never have made it. While she was behind Zach, she fetched her pill bottle and got a third aspirin out.

They reached the high pasture forty-five minutes later. It was some of the most beautiful country Taylor had ever seen. The ridge they were on was surrounded by towering mountains, thick with trees. A natural creek ran right through the center of the corral, and the grass was like a brilliant green carpet.

Four of the fence posts were down, and the cow trap leaned precariously, with one of the heavy wooden posts pulled almost out of the ground.

"We'll start on that after we fix camp," he said, indicating the trap.

Taylor was grateful to dismount. Before anything else, she walked Paladin into the corral, took off his saddle, blanket and bridle, then tied him with a long lead. He'd be comfortable all night, with fresh water and as much grass as he could eat. She petted him for a bit, stroking his warm neck. He was more interested in eating, though, so she left him there. Zach had gone through the same ritual with Falcon, and he put his saddle on the fence right next to Taylor's.

"What do you want me to do?" she asked.

"Set out your bed. Get some water. We'll eat lunch, then you can help with the fence posts until it's time to cook dinner." His eyes narrowed a bit. "You can cook, can't you?"

"I can."

"Good."

He left her again, and she thought about her article. How could she convey the difference between what most people thought of a cowboy's silence, and the real thing? Most people, accustomed to seeing cowboys in the movies, only imagined that a cowboy was quiet because he was thoughtful—intelligent, but frugal with his words. They imagined that when a cowboy did speak, it was something worth hearing. But she knew better. Zach wasn't any philosophy-spouting cowboy poet. He was just stubborn and uncommunicative.

Sighing, she resigned herself to a quiet couple of days, and unbuckled her bedroll from her saddle. By the time she had finished with her bed preparations, and filled four canteens with water, Zach was already working hard. She took the sandwiches Pearl had packed, and they ate standing right there. Zach didn't say anything at all to her, and she wished like crazy that Frankie could be here to see it. A man had to work hard at being this irascible. But Zach made it look easy.

When they finished eating, Zach got right back to work, and she pitched in. She certainly couldn't complain that he coddled her because she was a female. On the contrary. After just one hour, she was hot, sweaty and a whole battery of new muscles were sore. Zach, on the other hand, had a small sheen of sweat on his brow. Period. She hated that.

Finally, as the sun hit the tops of the mountain peaks, Zach called it a day. He went off to start a fire, while she excused herself to get cleaned up. The cold water of the stream felt wonderful, and if Zach hadn't been there she'd have stripped and taken a proper bath. As it was, she managed to get herself clean, if not refreshed. She even changed clothes in record time when Zach had his back turned.

She joined him by the fire and looked at the array of foods spread out by his side. Biscuits, stew that had been wrapped in some kind of reflective bag to keep it cold, apples and, to her surprise, a bottle of red wine.

Zach put a skillet on the fire to heat up, then handed her a thermos. "Coffee," he said. "Should still be reasonably warm."

"Thanks," she said, taking the top off. It was black, and still steaming. She poured herself a cup, then found a rock to sit on. To her relief, it didn't hurt too much. The aspirins were doing their job.

"You surprised me," Zach said.

"Pardon?"

"I said, you surprised me. You didn't complain at all."

"Complain about what?"

He looked at her, a little confusion showing up in the worry lines on his forehead. "I know you're sore as hell. But you didn't ask to stop but once on the ride up, and you didn't beg off from any of the heavy work. Most women would have…"

"Bitched?"

He nodded. "Yep."

She shook her head. "I think you don't know a great many women," she said. "We're not genetically programmed to complain. Honest."

"But a woman like you…"

"A woman like me? How would you know what kind of woman I am?"

Zach studied the fire for a moment before turning her way again. "Tell me."

"Tell you what?"

"You're right. I don't know you well. But we have the whole night ahead of us. So go on."

"I'm the one that's supposed to be interviewing you, remember?"

"Okay. Fair enough. You ask me a question, and I'll ask you one."

She nodded. "Deal. I go first."

"Okay." He turned back to the skillet and dumped

the stew in. The sizzle made her hungry even before the smell hit her. All that work had made her ravenous.

"Well?" he said. "You gonna ask or what?"

"Okay," she said. "What happened to you to make you so afraid of women?"

His mouth dropped open a bit. "So we're taking the gloves off, are we?" he said.

"I don't write fluff pieces, Zach."

"I see."

"So?"

He stirred the stew. "I want to say I'm not afraid of women, but I don't know if that would be the truth. I am afraid of them. Or at least what happens to men when they get around a woman they want."

"I'm not talking theory," she said. "Or about men in general. I want to know what happened to you."

"It didn't happen to me. It happened to one of my boys."

"Go on."

"I used to let girls on the ranch, same as boys. But the boys were just hitting that time in their lives when girls mattered more than anything. They'd show off, try fancy riding, getting on horses that weren't ready to be ridden. That kind of thing. It got out of hand, and some people got hurt."

"What happened?"

"At first, it wasn't much. A broken foot here, a strained wrist there. I chalked it up to the boys being young and not used to working on a ranch. But it didn't end there."

Taylor nodded, afraid that if she said anything, he'd stop talking.

"The worst of it happened five years back. A young kid, he was only fifteen, got thrown. He broke his back."

Taylor winced. "Oh, God. That's awful."

"He's a quadriplegic now. Because I didn't think things through. I should have known something like that would happen eventually."

"Surely you can't blame yourself. It was an accident."

"It was my ranch. My responsibility."

"No. It was an accident. That might have happened even if there had been no girls on the ranch."

"You're entitled to your opinion. But it's still my ranch. And as long as it is, there won't be any more girls." He reached over and picked up the bottle of wine. "You care for some?"

She nodded. "That would be nice."

He pulled a Swiss Army knife out of his pocket, then opened the bottle with a little *pop*. She handed him her empty thermos cup, and he filled it halfway. Then he took his own cup and did the same. After he took a sip, he gave her that crooked grin she was beginning to know. "My turn," he said.

"Shoot."

"Why are you using my ranch, and me, to get back at that guy who ran out on you?"

Chapter Six

Zach watched her carefully. His question had taken her by surprise, that much he could see. Her eyes widened, her mouth opened a little, and she drew in a sharp breath. But was that just because he'd surprised her by knowing something about her life, or had he really hit on the truth?

"What are you talking about?" she asked, shifting her gaze from his face to the fire.

He had the feeling that if he pressed her, he'd have to confess to listening to her conversation with Pearl. Which he didn't want to do. "Nothing. Forget it."

She looked back at him. "Too late. What did you mean?"

"Nothing. Just a guess. But it's still my turn," he said. "Tell me about this article you're writing. Is it really just about what a cowboy does with his days? You've been around ranches enough to know that without coming out here. So what's the real story going to be?"

She shifted uncomfortably, but he didn't think it was because she was sore.

"Is it about equal rights or something?" he asked. "Is that why you're always asking me about women on the ranch?"

She sighed, and he suspected he'd let her off the hook. Which meant he was right the first time. She was still carrying a grudge. What had that cowboy of hers done to her?

"It's not about equal rights. Not really. It's about telling the truth."

Zach stirred the stew, then handed Taylor the roll of tinfoil and a plastic bag with biscuits in it. "Wrap about four of those in foil," he said. "Then we'll heat them up."

She started on the task, while he turned his attention back to the skillet. "The truth, huh?" he said. "What truth would that be?"

She didn't speak for a minute, just folded the tinfoil around the biscuits. Then she put the packet on the fire. "There are a lot of misconceptions floating around about cowboys," she said finally. "Mostly gathered from movies and books."

"For example?"

"Well, that all cowboys are really Gary Cooper. Except for the ones in the black hats, of course."

"No one believes that, Taylor," he said. "People are smart enough to realize that being a cowboy is a job, just like any other."

"Oh, don't you believe it," she said. "There is a

tremendous mythology about cowboys. A mythology that has very little to do with real life."

"Go on."

"I read a book a little while ago. About a man on a ranch who had an almost mystical ability to understand woman. He was a typical, quiet man, of course. More comfortable on a horse than in a car. But somehow, his communing with the animals made him heroic. Gave him abilities no mere mortal could have."

"That's just a book. Fiction."

"But don't you see? That book was popular because it reinforced the concepts ingrained in us from watching Gary Cooper and John Wayne. It has nothing to do with the truth."

"So what? There are lots of things in the world that are romanticized. It doesn't hurt anyone."

"Of course it does," she said vehemently. "Women have this crazy notion that cowboys are better than normal men, and then they get trapped into a life they don't understand. It's not fair, and it's not right. Someone needs to set the record straight."

"And that would be you?"

"Yes. That would be me."

He took the skillet off the fire and reached for some paper plates. After serving her a sizable portion, he fetched the biscuit packet and opened it up. He put two on her plate, then passed it over. "What makes you so sure you know the truth?" he asked.

She sipped her wine, then put the cup down. "I told you before. I was raised on a ranch."

"So you had the universal experience? What you went through is what all women will go through?"

"No. But I've been through enough to see patterns of behavior. Not based on one person, but on a lot of people."

"Ten? Twenty? A hundred?"

"I don't know how many exactly. Enough."

"I think your idea of the truth is pretty damn narrow," he said as he fixed his own plate.

"As narrow as restricting your ranch to boys only after one accident?"

He stopped. "It's not the same thing."

When she didn't respond, he looked at her. He detected a little smug smile just before she bit into her biscuit. As if she'd won. But she hadn't.

She'd said that this was his playground, and she'd been correct. There was no way he was going to let her use his ranch for target practice. If she wanted to write an article about how cowboys were bastards, she was going to have to find another cowboy to do it with.

He ate then, but he didn't stop watching her. She barely met his eye, glancing instead at her plate, or at the mountains. In this light—golden, full of shadows as the sun paraded its colors before leaving for the night—Taylor looked mysterious and enigmatic. She reminded him of a coral snake, its very beauty announcing its danger to the world. He had done the right thing, bringing her with him. Keeping her away from the boys. Because if he was still attracted to her colors when he understood that she was dangerous, none of his young men would have stood a chance.

What he needed to do was stop thinking about her as a woman. She didn't have it right about him. He had a great deal of respect for females. He'd seen the things men did to impress them, to keep them, to win them. There was very little in nature that he respected more. So why did he suddenly want her? Why was he so aware of how her hair curved on her shoulder? Of the way her T-shirt stretched across her breasts? And why did he want to ignore everything he knew for one taste of her?

"Zach?"

"Yes?"

"Why did you bring me up here?"

"To give you your interview."

"I still want to go on the drive."

"I know."

"But you don't want me to, do you?"

"No."

"It's not because you don't think I can do the work, though, is it?"

"Nope. I've watched you. You're very capable. The way you have Paladin acting like a show pony hasn't escaped me. But no, you're not going on the drive."

"So you did bring me up here to keep the boys safe."

"That's right."

"What can I do to change your mind?"

"Nothing."

"Zach, I promised my editors that I'd be on the drive. They don't want to hear about us fixing fences."

"I'm sorry about that."

She put her plate down and stood up. He thought she was going off to pout in the woods, but all she did was get her sweatshirt and his jacket. She came back and sat down right next to him. "Thought you might be chilly, too," she said, handing him the jacket, then slipping the sweatshirt on.

"Thanks."

"It's very beautiful here," she said. "Did I tell you I saw an eagle? When I was filling the canteen?"

"There are a lot of eagles out here. Hawks, too."

She didn't say anything for a few minutes, and Zach thought she might be trying to figure out a way to talk about going on the drive again.

"So what do you normally do at night up here?"

Okay, so he was wrong. For now. He picked up her plate and his and put them in a large trash bag. Then he put a pan of water on the fire so she wouldn't have to wash up at the cold creek. "Play cards. Tell lies."

"That sounds good," she said. "Well, maybe not the lies part."

He smiled. "You want the real cowboy experience, don't you?"

She wasn't sharing his joke. "I've had a lifetime of cowboy lies," she said. "If that's all you have to offer, I think I'll pass."

There it was again. The reference to the man who

left her. He was curious about what happened, but he wouldn't ask. She'd tell him what she wanted him to know. "I'll get the cards," he said. "Why don't you pour us each a little more wine."

He got up and put on his jacket, then went to his bedroll and picked up the old deck of cards he always kept with him. The sun had dipped behind the horizon, but it wasn't completely dark yet. He took his flashlight with him back to the fire, then sat down across from Taylor.

They wouldn't play long. She'd had a rough day, and tomorrow was going to be rougher. What they needed now was to lighten up. "You know how to play gin?"

"Of course," she said. "What are we playing for?"

"Stakes, eh?"

"I know," she said. "I win, I go on the drive. You win, we talk about it some more."

He laughed. "You're a devious creature," he said.

"Devious? No way. Just determined."

"Let's play for who has to make coffee in the morning."

"Deal."

"Before we start, it's going to get cold, and it's already getting dark. Why don't you bring your sleeping bag in a little closer, and if you want to wash up, now would be the time."

"Good idea," she said. She stood, wincing a little and putting her hand on her backside.

It wasn't so dark that he couldn't see her. He leaned

back against a rock and watched her putter at her bed-roll. Her silhouette had him thinking forbidden thoughts. Couldn't he look at her for five minutes without thinking of sex? Standing abruptly, he went over to her side, fighting the urge to touch her. "Let me set up your bed," he said, needing her to leave before he did something stupid. "The water's hot. Go get washed up."

By the time she was finished, he'd squared her stuff away so that when she was ready she could just crawl in her bag and go to sleep. He'd also calmed down a bit, but it was clear tonight wasn't going to be easy. Even though his gear was on the other side of the fire, he had a feeling there was no safe distance from her.

It was nuts. It's not as if she was the first woman he'd seen in years. He wasn't desperate. Just a few weeks ago he'd spent some quality time with his old friend Karen. So why was he so fixated? What was it about Taylor that made him so hungry for her?

She was attractive, sure, but he'd been with other attractive women before and he hadn't gone on like this. She was a challenge, but again, he'd been with challenging women. He couldn't remember a time when he'd reacted this way. If he could figure it out, maybe he could stop it. The only thing he was sure about was the fact that he didn't *want* to want her.

When she came back to her seat by the fire, he'd put her sleeping bag close so she could sit on it, rather than the cold ground. "You ready?" she asked.

He answered her by shuffling the cards. She picked

up her thermos cup and sipped her wine. "I'd forgotten how dark the night can be," she said. "How bright the stars are. That was one of my favorite things growing up. Crawling into a nice warm sleeping bag and staring up at the stars. They're not the same in the city. I don't even notice them there."

"Good reason not to live in the city."

She picked up her hand and arranged her cards.

"So what else did you like about growing up on the ranch?" he asked, shifting his own hand.

"Riding. I love horses. I miss that."

"Aren't there stables in Houston?"

"Yes, but I don't have a lot of time. My weeks are pretty busy, and I'm usually working on the weekends."

"Not dating? Going to fancy restaurants and nightclubs?"

"Me? I'm not much of a nightclub person."

"So what kind of a person are you?"

She concentrated on the game for a bit. "I like movies," she said finally. "The symphony. Plays. Although I don't get to them as often as I'd like. I'm pretty into politics, too. Eventually, I'd like to be a political columnist, but that's not going to be for a while. I cover some local elections now. So that means spending time at city hall. Being a writer isn't nine-to-five work. I have dinner with friends at least once a week. I go to the gym. Boy, it doesn't sound too exciting, does it?"

"It sounds okay," he said. He picked a card from the deck, then laid his hand down. "Gin."

"One to nothing," she said. "What are we going to play to?"

"Five out of seven?"

"Okay." She got the deck together and shuffled.

"No boyfriend?" he said, hoping his voice sounded casual.

"Nope. Not at the moment."

"Pretty thing like you, I'd imagine you'd be beating them off with a stick."

She laughed. "You need to get out more."

"I'm serious," he said.

She looked up from the cards—just looked at him for a long moment. "Thank you," she said, her voice just above a whisper.

Another clue. Zach was slowly building up a picture of Taylor, piece by piece. He wouldn't have guessed that she was insecure about her looks. Her confidence about her abilities was rock-solid. Perhaps another legacy of the fiancé who had left her?

Taylor dealt the next hand, and while they continued to play the conversation grew sparse. Zach didn't mind. He took the opportunity to quietly study the woman who upset his equilibrium just by being near.

IT WAS ONLY nine-fifteen, but Taylor was more than ready to go to bed. At least she didn't have to make coffee in the morning. Zach had been a good loser, but that hadn't surprised her. Although he took himself seriously, from what she'd been able to see, he wasn't a petty man. And although he had some strange notions about women, he didn't seem to be one of those men who had to keep proving he was better at everything.

She'd learned more from tonight's dinner and card game than she'd anticipated. Unfortunately, none of what she learned was going to make her article better. Zach wasn't a typical cowboy. He hadn't once brought up cows, horses, trucks, guns or ranching. She tried to recall an evening spent with her father or Ben or any of the cowboys she'd grown up around, during which at least one of those topics hadn't been chewed on for hours.

In fact, Zach had spent most of the evening listening to her. She knew he'd listened because he'd asked questions. Not arbitrary questions, either. Pertinent. Astute. Thoughtful. Three characteristics she'd never associated with a cowboy before.

She glanced over to the other side of the freshly banked fire to see the man in question zipping himself into his sleeping bag. She reached into her pack and got the inflatable pillow she always kept with her kit, and blew it up. It was one of her only serious indulgences when she went out on the range. That, and her perfume. The longer she was on a drive, the more important the perfume became. Not just because of the odor from the animals, but because there aren't many opportunities to shower on a cattle drive. She'd always managed, but the men hadn't seemed to think it was a priority.

She crawled into her sleeping bag, aware that she hadn't slept in her clothes in more than five years. There were so many things, details, she'd forgotten. Some were pleasant, but most were inconveniences that she hadn't missed in the least.

She shifted until she was comfortably on her stomach, facing the fire and Zach. From this angle, she couldn't tell if his eyes were closed or not. He faced her, too, and once more she thought about how he didn't fit her profile.

Oh, she hadn't forgotten his arrogance. Nothing about tonight had changed that in the least. But he was far more considerate than she'd ever have guessed. Little things, like putting the pot on the stove so she could wash with hot water, setting up her sleeping bag, offering her an extra blanket.

The truth was, she didn't completely dislike Zach. Not that he was a hero or anything. He just wasn't a total jerk. Maybe not even a jerk at all.

So what did that do to her article? She'd have to make some adjustments, but now that she thought about it, this could work to her advantage. By pointing out his good points, she could make it very clear that she was being totally fair. No one could accuse her of bias.

It didn't change anything, really. Not the fact that most women had no idea who they were getting involved with when they chose a cowboy. Not the fact that she had to stop her sister from making a huge mistake.

But if it turned out that Frankie decided to marry Cal no matter what, Taylor could take some small comfort in the fact that Cal was under the tutelage of a man like Zach. It could have been much worse.

She closed her eyes, exhausted, sore, but not unhappy. Actually, she was almost looking forward to tomorrow. Working with Zach would be interesting, if nothing else. Learning more about him intrigued her. And she had to face it, watching him wasn't exactly punishment.

What would it be like to kiss a man like Zach? She remembered the feel of him when she was rubbing the warmth back into his body. Nothing gave. He was solid with muscle and sinew. Masculine in a way that made her terribly aware of her own femininity.

That was it.

That was what had been swimming around outside her consciousness. What had made being with Zach so different.

All those years she'd spent on the ranch, she'd felt that being a girl was a deficit. One she could never overcome. Her father had made it clear that he'd wished she had been a boy. The cowboys had penalized her in a hundred ways for being different, softer. Even Ben had made it clear that while he found her reasonably attractive, he still preferred to spend time with his buddies.

Zach, for all his posturing about women on his

ranch, hadn't once made her feel inadequate because
she was female. She remembered his compliment
about her looks. From what she could tell, he'd actually meant it. That shouldn't have made any difference,
but it did. She was glad that he liked the way she
looked. That he noticed at all.

Why? Surely, she wasn't interested in him *that* way.
No. He was a cowboy. Even if he did have the body
of a David and the face of a movie star. He was still
a cowboy, and that meant nothing but trouble.

So she'd better stop thinking about the way he
looked in those jeans of his. And the broadness of his
shoulders. And his crooked little smile. And she'd certainly better not think about the hunger in his eyes.

Chapter Seven

Taylor finally figured it out. They should get rid of all the gyms in the world, and make people work on a ranch if they wanted to get in shape.

Zach had awakened her at sunrise. He'd made the coffee, as promised, but he'd also made breakfast while she was busy getting herself cleaned up and dressed. All the while, she was thinking about the dreams she'd had the night before. Dreams of Zach. Not one of them G-rated. The one she remembered most clearly had them back at the waterfall, only this time there was no blanket to warm him. Only her hands, and her body. She blushed just thinking about it.

She'd come back to the fire, and Zach had heated some more biscuits, cooked oatmeal, eggs and bacon. She ate much more than usual, knowing what kind of day she was going to have.

She should have eaten more.

Lifting logs that each weighed more than a Buick; pounding nails that refused to go in properly until

she'd hit her thumb at least once; chopping wood...
And watching Zach, who accomplished each task so
easily that by noon she was ready to shoot him.

She had to give him credit, though. He was very
considerate of her, always making sure she wasn't doing more than she was capable of. But she never let
on that the pain in the muscles of her upper body completely eclipsed the pain in her posterior. Nothing a
few months in a hospital wouldn't fix.

She approached the last of the fence posts that had
been damaged. Once this was repaired, they were going to take a break for lunch. Then they'd work on the
triggers, but that job shouldn't take long.

The whole contraption was just a way to make the
cows enter the corral one at a time, so they could be
counted and vaccinated. But with the triggers and the
wire pulls, and the heavy, heavy logs, everything had
to fit together smoothly and solidly enough so the cows
wouldn't be able to knock it over.

She squatted to get hold of the log.

"Hey!"

She looked up. Zach stood just a few feet away.
That he could look so good after doing all that labor
was completely unfair. "Yeah?"

"I can get that."

"No, it's okay. I've got it."

He walked toward her, shaking his head and giving
her that half smile that had bothered her in her dreams.
"You've proved your point, Wonder Woman. I know
you can work as hard as any man. But the basic truth

is that men have more upper-body strength. Not my fault, you understand. Just the truth.''

She stood up, careful not to wince as her thighs screamed in pain. "And?"

"And I made breakfast, so it's your turn to cook."

That, she couldn't argue with. But it still rankled that he'd done twice the work she had. "Tell you what. Let's do this together, and then we'll both take a break."

"Anyone ever mention that you can be stubborn?"

She nodded. "Just about everyone who knows me."

"And you've felt no need to do something about it?"

She smiled as she wiped her forehead with her arm. "Nope. It's worked quite well for me, thank you."

"Well, I guess I can understand that." He moved in close, taking her place next to the log. "What I don't understand is why you gave up ranching when you like it so much."

"Me? Like it? Whatever gave you that idea?"

He didn't answer her right away. First, he centered himself, then hoisted the log to slip it back where it belonged. Taylor quickly moved out of the way, and saw that he didn't need her help at all. He got the log lined up, then shoved it into position. Then he turned to her, not even breathing heavily from the exertion. "You've been singing all morning. I haven't figured out the song yet, but it isn't a dirge."

"I have not."

He nodded.

Then she thought about it. There had been a song stuck in her head all day, but she hadn't realized she'd been humming. She knew she hadn't actually sung out loud, though. "Is that the universal test?" she asked. "If a person hums while ranching, it means they should drop everything and become a cowboy?"

Zach nodded again. "Yep. You got that right. First thing I do when I get a new hand is listen for the music."

"You're full of beans, mister."

He turned his head slightly left, then narrowed his eyes, keeping his gaze on her. "Wait a sec," he said. He took off his glove, then reached over with his hand and rubbed her cheek with his thumb.

"What?" she asked.

"You had a little dirt there." He took another step closer to her, and his hand went to her cheek again. This time, it wasn't his thumb that touched her but the back of his hand. Just a slight brush, gentle as the wind.

"Still dirty?" she asked, surprised that she couldn't catch her breath when she'd been standing idle for so long.

"Nope," he whispered.

She didn't know what to say. All she could do was stare into his eyes, searching for something, some explanation as to why her heart beat so rapidly.

"I lied, you know," he said, his voice just above a whisper.

"Did you?"

He nodded slowly. "I recognized your song right away."

"Oh?"

"'Love Me Tender.' That's it, isn't it?"

She swallowed, then just as she was about to nod, he moved those last few inches and kissed her.

He took her completely by surprise, and yet her arms curled around his neck as if she'd been waiting for this moment all her life. Her body softened against his, feeling the hardness of the man from her chest all the way down. Even as the realization hit her that she was kissing a cowboy—the last thing in the world she should ever do—Zach's kiss deepened, and all her good sense vanished with the taste of him.

His arms went around her, touching her at the small of her back, pulling her closer. She heard his deep moan as his tongue slipped between her teeth. It was a perfect kiss, a dreamy, princess-awakening kiss that roused a need inside her. A need she hadn't known she had.

She wanted to touch him everywhere, and to feel him touch her right back. She moved her hips and ran her fingers through his hair, knocking his hat straight off his head. She didn't care, and he didn't miss a beat.

He just kept kissing her. Making her groan. Making her wet.

When he pulled back, she was breathless.

"Wow," he whispered as his gaze captured hers.

"Yeah," she said, her own voice shaky and soft.

"I didn't know I was going to do that," he said.

"Yeah," she said again, unable to form anything more coherent.

"The thing is, I liked it," he said. He moved his hand over her back, keeping her plastered to his body. "A lot."

She almost said, "Yeah," again. Then her brain engaged. "You're a cowboy," she said, releasing her hold on him. "I can't do this."

He didn't let her go. "Why not?"

"Because I know you. I know what you want. I can't give it to you."

"What do I want?" he asked.

She pushed against his chest, and he let her go. For a second, she wanted to rush back into the circle of his arms, but her good sense stopped her. "You don't want me."

"How the hell do you know?" he said, a hint of a growl just under his words.

"Because I won't play second banana to your ranch. I don't like this life. I don't want it."

"I didn't ask you to marry me," he said.

She felt her cheeks heat, and she turned away from him. "I know. It was just a kiss. But we have no business kissing."

"You sure didn't seem to mind."

"You caught me off guard, that's all."

"Right," he said. "Pardon me. I made a mistake. It won't happen again." He bent down and picked up his hat, then walked toward the campsite, hitting his hat sharply against his thigh.

She watched him go. She should have been pleased, but she wasn't. She wanted him back. At least a part of her did. The part that had gotten her into so much trouble before. For once in her life she wasn't going to listen. She was determined to do the smart thing, even if he *had* kissed her like she'd never been kissed before.

All that was happening here was hormones. Nothing more. It didn't mean she had to act on them. If she did, she'd never be able to warn Frankie off her cowboy. More important, she'd put herself right back into the position that had caused most of the pain in her life. It would be stupid. Crazy. Wrong.

If only she could get her head to communicate that message to her body. Something needed to quash the ache she felt. Of all the aches she'd felt since she'd come to the ranch, this was the deepest. It wouldn't be soothed by liniment or by sitting in a hot tub. This one could only be cured by one thing—distance and time. Getting away from the cause. But she couldn't just leave. She had to do the article.

The article. That was it. She'd write it all out, see in black and white the folly of wanting him. By the time she finished her piece, she'd know that Zach was the last person in the world she should be with. That he was everything she needed to avoid. That even his kisses weren't worth the price she'd have to pay.

ZACH WORKED on the triggers while Taylor fixed lunch, cursing under his breath the whole time. What kind of a mule-brained idiot was he? Of all the fool things in the world he could have done, kissing Taylor was the most foolish.

He knew perfectly well how she felt about him, and his life, and his ranch. About men, specifically cowboys. He didn't particularly like her opinions, or her stubbornness. So what in hell had he been thinking?

She'd tricked him. She'd set him up. How come she insisted on wearing those tight jeans? Or those T-shirts? Didn't she know she was just asking for trouble when she looked that good? And what about all that nice talk last night? Those smiles? That laugh? What was that all about, if not to make him drop his defenses?

Women. They screwed him up every time.

He pounded the wire on the last of the traps, then tested the gate. It worked fine.

He looked back at the camp. Taylor sat by the fire, stirring something in the skillet. A wave of lust came over him, quicker than a flash flood in a canyon. He turned away, cursing his luck. Why *his* ranch? Why *him?*

Everything had been great until she'd shown up. It was Pearl's fault. She'd invited Taylor. He'd give his aunt a piece of his mind when he got back.

He risked another glance at Taylor, and when he turned, she waved at him. Lunch was ready. He didn't want to eat with her. Or sit near her. Or look her way. He didn't want to feel this horrible pull in his gut, or the need that took his senses.

He looked at his watch: eleven-fifteen. They'd head back by one, and make it to the ranch by nightfall. Thank God. He couldn't take another night with her out here. With his thoughts. With his body reacting to her the way it did.

After he swung the gate a couple more times, just to make sure the hinges worked, he headed back. He had to eat. And why shouldn't he? This was his playground, wasn't it? He made the rules. It was his way or the highway. He wasn't going to think about her as anything but a reporter. A visitor who'd be gone by tomorrow.

That helped him to breathe easily again. One more day. One more night. Piece of cake.

"I made the rest of the stew," she said, when he reached the campsite. "And some sandwiches, too. I wasn't sure what you'd like."

"That's fine," he said.

"You want coffee?"

He nodded, not daring to look at her.

She served him up a plate of stew and put a sandwich on top. He sat himself down on a rock and started eating. He heard her sigh, then the sound of her scraping at the skillet. But he didn't look. He wouldn't.

"So how long is it going to take us to finish up with the triggers?" she asked.

"Not long," he said. "Another hour or two, then we'll go back. You can start packing after lunch." He ate some more, not tasting the food at all. He hated the awkwardness he felt. It was a very new, very uncomfortable sensation. He couldn't remember being this itchy, at least not since he was a teenager.

It wasn't as if he hadn't played his card to a closed deck before. He'd shrugged it off as a miscalculation and moved on. No regrets. But not with *her*.

"You're angry with me."

He stopped chewing. Swallowed. "No, I'm not."

"Yes, you are. You can't even look at me."

He turned and stared right at her. "Feel better?"

"No. I didn't mean to imply that stopping the… It wasn't personal."

He laughed. "Right."

"It wasn't. Now be fair. You know as well as I do that we shouldn't… That it couldn't go anywhere. I'm leaving after the drive. Going back to where I belong."

"First," he said, putting his plate down and turning his body to face hers, "you're not going on the drive. Second, you don't know *where* you belong."

She sat up straighter. "What does that mean?"

"It means you aren't going on the drive."

"You know what I'm talking about. How do you know anything about where I belong?"

"Just stating the obvious."

"Obvious? To whom?"

"Me. Pearl. Probably everyone else you know."

"God, you are so typical. I won't sleep with you, so now I'm just a confused female who doesn't know what she wants. I suppose you think what I really want is *you?* Well, I've got news for you Cowboy Bob—I don't want you. I barely like you. And that doesn't have anything to do with the fact that you're just exactly the kind of man that I've learned to avoid.''

She stood up, still holding her paper plate in one hand and her sandwich in the other. "For your information, I've lived around your kind my whole life. From my father on up. I even made the hideous mistake of thinking I was in love with one of you. Ha! How could I love someone who wasn't there? Someone who thought his horse was more important than his girlfriend? Who believed the only thing a woman was good for was cooking, cleaning and having babies. Well, you can all go to hell!"

She found the trash bag and shoved her plate and unfinished sandwich inside. Then she stomped over to her sleeping bag and started rolling it up.

Zach stood and walked over to where she was crouching on the ground. "I'll tell you something, Missy. You won't know what you want until you start seeing people as individuals. Until you realize that you're judging all the men in the world based on a mistake *you* made. What you need to do is grow the hell up.''

Before she could respond, he headed back to the corral. One good thing had happened. He wasn't angry at himself anymore. He was angry at her.

TAYLOR COULDN'T form the words that she wanted to yell at Zach as he walked away from her. She just sputtered and got more frustrated until finally she did the only thing she could think to do. She kicked his bedroll as hard as she could. It didn't work. Not even a little. It was his behind she wanted at the end of her boot, not his sleeping bag.

Imagine him telling her that she needed to grow up! The man surrounded himself with *teenagers*. Probably couldn't get adults to work with him.

God, she was furious! If she'd had any idea how to get back to the ranch, she would have climbed on Paladin this instant and ridden back. The hell with the article. The hell with Zach! She finished rolling up her bag, and then quickly got her pack ready to load on her horse.

She was just getting the cooking supplies together so she could wash them, when she heard his shout.

Dropping the pan, she ran toward the corral. That had been a shout of pain. Severe pain. A sound a man like Zach wouldn't make unless he was truly hurt. And there was the proof: him sitting on the grass with the top log from the trigger frame leaning next to him. The log had to be at least a hundred pounds!

But, he was sitting up. If he could sit, he could still breathe.

She tore through the gate and rushed to his side. "What's wrong? What happened?"

He was rubbing the back of his neck. His hat lay upside down on the ground next to him. Other than that, he looked perfectly okay. Except for the grimace.

"Nothing. I'm fine."

"You are not. Tell me what happened!"

He winced as he kept rubbing. "The damn log wasn't secured properly. It fell on me."

"On your back?"

He nodded, but stopped short. "Yes. It's fine. Go on. Finish packing."

"No way. You're coming with me." She reached down for his free hand.

He looked up at her, hesitant, but finally he took it, and let her pull him to his feet. She knew he was hurting when *she* had to grab his hat. He didn't walk with a limp, but still she kept close, afraid he'd keel over any second. She desperately tried to remember her first aid. But the only thing she could think of was give him aspirin, and rub his back with liniment. Thank goodness she hadn't used it all up.

"Quit looking at me like that. I told you, I'm fine."

"We'll see," she said.

They got back to the campsite, and Zach stopped when he saw his sleeping bag twisted and his blanket strewn across the grass. She hurried in front of him and straightened it all out, then went back and took his hand once more. "Come on, big guy. Let's see the damage."

He let her lead him to his bedroll, then he sat, moaning as he touched down.

"Wait here," she said. She went to her pack and got the bottle of aspirin and the ointment. By the time she got back to him, he was taking off his shirt. He moved so gingerly she was sure he needed more help than she could give him.

She didn't see anything wrong until she stood right in front of him. A bruise was forming on his left shoulder and back. It looked nasty and painful. "Here," she said, giving him the bottle. Then she found his canteen and handed that to him. "I don't think three aspirins are going to help much."

"That's why I'm going to take four."

"Are you sure it's safe?"

He started to nod, but that seemed to hurt a lot. "I'm sure. Look, this is nothing. I've hurt myself lots worse than this breaking horses."

"I wouldn't doubt it. But that was then, and now you're with me, and I'm going to do something about that bruise right now." She went in back of him and knelt down.

"What?" he asked, leaning forward as if warning her not to touch.

"I'm going to beat you about the head and shoulders. What do you think? I'm just putting on some liniment. We don't have any ice to slow the swelling, so this'll have to do."

"Okay," he said grudgingly. "But be careful."

She opened up the tube and spread some of the thick ointment on her hands. As gently as possible, she started to rub his back. He gasped when she touched him, and then he was silent, even though she knew it had to hurt.

He moaned, and she winced for him. The red parts were turning blue, and the blue parts were turning purple. Nice colors for a sunset, but for a back? She didn't like it.

She finished up, then reached for his shirt. She helped him put it on, which seemed to be a little more difficult than he'd anticipated, from the look of him.

She got up, went to her bedroll, and spread it out again. Then she took her pillow and joined Zach once more. "Here," she said. "You can probably use this more than me."

"What for?"

"To sleep on, what do you think?"

"We're not staying here tonight."

"Want to bet?"

Chapter Eight

Zach couldn't believe what a fool he was. He'd been careless. If one of his boys had done this, Zach would have given him hell. And then some.

One thing was crystal clear, though. He'd been absolutely correct about Taylor. She was a distraction of the first order.

He shouldn't have let her get to him. He shouldn't have kissed her. No matter how he looked at it, though, he was the one to blame, not her. It was up to him to be strong, to ignore her curves and her smile. Her lips. But he hadn't, had he? Now he was stuck up here another day...

"No," he said. "We're not staying. I'm bruised but I can ride just fine."

"Are you crazy?" she asked. "If we were near town, I'd take you to the hospital. How do you know you haven't broken anything?"

He slowly flexed his shoulders. It hurt, but it wasn't the kind of hurt that comes from broken bones. He knew, having broken so many. "You have more aspirin?" he asked.

"Another bottle."

"Can you finish cleaning up here?"

She nodded, even though he could see that she didn't want to do it.

"Then we go. I'll be better off back at the ranch."

Taylor put her hands on her hips and shook her head once more. "What if something *is* busted? You could hurt yourself a lot worse."

He put his right hand on his sleeping bag and pushed himself up. It wasn't fun, but he did his best not to show it. "I appreciate the concern," he said, "but I swear, I'm okay."

"It's *your* body," she said, turning back to the skillet she'd dropped. "Far be it from me to tell you how to run your life. I'm not your mother. I don't care that the cattle drive is less than a week away. I'm not the one who's going to suffer."

"Taylor," he said.

"What?" She turned to him, scowling.

"If it's bad, we'll stop. Okay?"

She looked him over from head to toe, then back up again. "Promise?"

He nodded. Carefully.

"I'll finish up here. You go find yourself a nice rock to sit on."

"I can—"

"Do you have to argue with everything?"

He smiled. "Yep."

"Why do I bother?" she said, sighing dramatically.

He decided it was easier just to let her have her way. *This* time. He found a big rock to lean against, and then he systematically stretched the muscles in his arms, shoulders and back, gauging the pain while he increased the circulation. But he kept his gaze on Taylor.

She worked efficiently and quietly. He admired that. Except for her stubbornness, and her opinions, there were quite a few things he admired about her. Although wild mustangs couldn't make him admit that to her.

She was different from most of the women he knew. Actually, she kind of reminded him of a mustang. Headstrong, beautiful, wild.

What the hell was he doing? The woman disliked everything he stood for. She hated ranching and she hated cowboys. Since he wasn't about to give up either one, thinking about her didn't accomplish anything except to get him upset.

For the next half hour, he concentrated on anything but Taylor. He went through his mental list of all he had to accomplish before the drive. That reminded him that he'd promised Johnny that he'd work with him on his roping. How was he going to do that when his shoulder was banged up like this? He'd think of something. Damn his careless hide.

"I think that does it," Taylor said, wiping her brow with her arm.

He walked over to the campsite and saw that she'd done everything. Packed him up, buried the fire, made sure there was no trash. She'd even saddled Paladin and Falcon. "Thanks," he said.

A momentary flash of disappointment marred her features, but then she smiled again. It made her look as fresh and pretty as the sky above her.

She walked with him to Falcon. "Come on," she said. "Let's get you mounted."

He almost told her to forget it, but then he thought about the muscles needed to mount the horse. Riding, he could do. He'd just favor the left arm. This part wasn't so easy.

"Well? I thought you wanted to get a move on."

He sucked it up and moved into position. Grabbing the saddle horn with his right hand, he put his boot in the stirrup, but then he hesitated.

"Ready?"

In answer, he pulled himself up, the pain hitting immediately. Then he felt her hands on his backside, shoving him up and over the saddle. "Hey!"

"What was I supposed to grab on to?" she asked gruffly. When he looked at her though, she was smiling smugly.

"There were several other places that you could have grabbed."

"But they wouldn't have been half as much fun."

She laughed as she went over to Paladin. Zach smiled. The woman might be dangerous, but she sure sounded nice when she laughed.

THEY REACHED the ranch just before eight. Bone tired and achy, Taylor could hardly imagine how Zach must be feeling. Of course he hadn't complained. That would be against the cowboy code. What he had done was talk. Mostly about his childhood and how he'd come to love being a cowboy. Of course, he hadn't said it quite that way. But with each anecdote, he'd told of his love for the land, his pride in his stock, his disdain for any life other than his own.

He'd spoken so eloquently, with such conviction, that she'd almost found herself wishing she hadn't left her ranch home. Almost.

The reality was that Zach's stories were only a tiny view into a much broader window. He'd left out all the awful parts which, she knew from experience, greatly outnumbered the good parts.

But he had reminded her of glorious days. When the air felt as crisp as a Granny Smith apple, and the sky went on forever and ever. When she'd felt so connected to the land around her, she'd lost the ability to speak.

That was a long time ago. Remembered through the haze of distance. Exaggerated through dreams and disappointments.

As they stepped into the house and Taylor got a good look at Zach, she could see the pain etched in his face. All she wanted to do now was take a long, hot shower and go to bed. Instead, she turned to Zach. "Hey. You think you can manage to take off your clothes by yourself?"

He tried to grin at her, but wasn't very successful. "Why, is that an offer?"

"You bet your ass it is."

He started to reach over with his left hand, presumably to touch her, but the motion was stillborn. "I can manage."

"Then this is what we're going to do. You climb into your swim trunks and then toddle out to the hot tub. I'm going to grab us some food and drink, and I'll meet you out there."

"I don't know. I'm pretty tired. I think I'm just gonna go lay down."

"Absolutely not. If you think you're sore now, you just ignore it and see what you feel like tomorrow."

"All right," he said. "But on one condition."

"What?"

"You climb into that old hot tub with me."

"Try and stop me. I hurt from here to Sunday. Now, go on. I'll meet you there." She left him at the foot of the stairs and headed for the kitchen.

"Taylor."

She stopped. Turned. "Yeah?"

"You gonna wear that bathing suit you had on the other night?"

She shook her head. "I swear. You men. You could be on your deathbed and you'd still try to look up an angel's skirt."

He laughed. Taylor liked that. She went toward the kitchen, and heard Pearl's voice before she walked through the door to find the older woman with one of Zach's boys.

"What are you doing back so early?" Pearl asked.

"Zach had an accident. Don't worry, he seems

okay. Just sore. I thought I'd fix him something to eat. I've got him changing so he can get into the hot tub.''

Pearl turned to the young man standing by the open fridge.

"Eddie, go on out and make sure the hot tub is on, would you?"

He nodded, smiled brightly at Taylor, then hurried out.

"Watch out for him," Pearl said as soon as the door closed behind him. "He likes practical jokes. Don't be surprised to find a rubber snake in your sleeping bag some night."

"From the way Zach's been talking, Eddie won't have the chance."

Pearl reached into the refrigerator and pulled out a big covered pot. "Tell me what happened to him. We can discuss the drive in a minute."

Taylor eased into a chair, still smarting madly from riding so much. The way she felt tonight, she wouldn't mind not going on the drive. All she really wanted was to feel good again.

"I made pot roast," Pearl said, "potatoes, carrots and peas. That okay with you?"

"It sounds like heaven. But I should help."

"You sit still."

Pearl didn't have to ask her twice. "One of the logs from the trap frame came off and hit him in the back," she explained. "It's a nasty bruise, but he insists nothing's broken."

"He'd know. He's broken most everything at one time or another."

"Still, I wish he'd see a doctor."

Pearl turned on the burner underneath the pot, then went back to the fridge for more. "He's not a foolish man," she said. "At least when it comes to his health. He'd go to the doctor if he needed to."

"I'm glad to hear that."

Pearl, holding a covered casserole dish, turned to her. "Which is not to say he's not a fool in other ways."

"Meaning?"

"This nonsense about you not going on the drive."

"Oh, yeah. He seems pretty determined to send me away."

"We'll see about that."

Taylor sighed. "I don't want to fight him the whole way."

"You won't have to." Pearl put the casserole in the oven. "Tell me something, Taylor. Did Zach talk to you while you were out there?"

"Yes, he did."

"I don't mean chitchat. I mean talk."

Taylor nodded.

"I figured he would. He doesn't do that with everyone, you know."

"Talk?"

"Yep. Even if he was out on the range for days at a time, if he didn't think a person was worth talking to, he just plain wouldn't."

"And I'm worth it?"

"Uh-huh. And honey, he's worth listening to."

"I listened."

"Did you?"

Taylor looked at Pearl, into her pale blue eyes. She clearly loved her nephew and thought highly of him.

"You know why I never married?" Pearl said, stepping closer and taking Taylor's hand in her own. "Because when the right man talked to me, I didn't know how to listen."

Taylor felt her cheeks heat, although she wasn't sure why. She didn't think it was because Pearl had revealed a secret. It was more the subtext of her message: the idea that Zach could be more than just the subject of an article. It was crazy, of course. Well, except for that kiss. She slipped her hand out of Pearl's. "I think when the right man comes around, I'll be ready."

"I hope so. Now why don't you go on upstairs and change so you can climb into that hot tub with Zach. I'll bring the food out to you."

Standing up was almost more difficult than sitting had been, but Taylor did it. Before she left, she went to Pearl and kissed her lightly on the cheek. "Thanks. For everything."

"I'm happy to help. Now go on. You look like you could use a good soak."

HE SAT FACING the sliding glass door, and it paid off. Taylor wore the bathing suit he liked so much. Her towel didn't even obscure too much of it, so he got to watch her cross the deck, put her things down on the bench, then come over to the tub.

"How are you feeling?" she asked as she climbed the few stairs.

"Better now that I'm not on a horse."

"Boy, do I hear that." She stepped into the water up to her waist, then waited a moment, probably adjusting to the temperature.

"You're still sore, eh?"

She nodded. "From top to toe. But it's not as bad as it was. I guess I'm getting used to it."

"Developing calluses, eh?"

She laughed. "I certainly hope not! Where I'm sore, calluses would be most inconvenient."

He smiled as he sank a little lower on his seat, allowing the hot water to soak his shoulders and neck. But his focus wasn't really on his back. It was on her. She was still only in up to her waist and he liked the way her one-piece suit hugged her body. Her breasts, cupped by the material, revealed that she was still chilly, because he could see her nipples in perfect definition. Maybe she'd stay like that for a while. Looking at her helped him forget about his aches.

Which proved yet again that Taylor Reed was a distraction. He had no doubt that he'd been careless because he'd been thinking about her. Angry that he'd made a fool of himself, and that she'd made it very clear she didn't want anything to do with him.

And yet, he still wanted her.

During the long, painful ride home, he'd come to grips with that. It wasn't as if he loved her or anything that severe. He just wanted her. Why not? She was a beautiful woman. Bright, articulate, a good cowhand.

Of course he was attracted to her. That didn't mean he had to do anything about it.

She sank lower in the water, then moved straight across from him and sat down. "Pearl's coming out with dinner," she said.

"I'm not hungry anymore."

"You should eat. It's been a taxing day."

"I know. But if it's a choice between moving, and staying put, I'm not moving."

"I can't argue too much with that. Whoever built this hot tub was very smart."

"It was Pearl's idea."

"Bless her."

Zach closed his eyes and concentrated on the warmth soothing his back. He drifted as he relaxed further, feeling the cool night air on his face, which made the water seem even hotter.

"Scoot up."

He opened his eyes to find Taylor right next to him. He hadn't heard her move. "Hmm?"

"Let me get behind you. Scoot up."

He moved forward until he just barely sat on the bench. Taylor moved behind him and slipped her legs down on either side of him. If he moved back an inch, he'd feel her breasts on his back.

She put her hands on his shoulders and gently, very gently, began to massage him. The feeling was indescribable. The combination of her closeness, the way her smooth legs brushed his, and the delicacy of her hands made him moan with pleasure.

"Am I hurting you?" she asked, stilling her hands.

"No, not at all. It's great."

She began again. Slow, even movements. When she moved lower on his back, he winced, but the pain was small and short-lived—and completely worth it.

He slipped forward a little, and went to grab hold of the bench, but he found a better purchase. He cupped the outside of her thighs. Tentatively at first, waiting for her to protest, but when she didn't, he let himself relax and enjoy it.

Something caught his attention at the sliding glass door. It had to be Pearl. He wanted to tell her not to come out. Food was the last thing on his mind. Hell, even if he were starving to death, he'd pass on a T-bone steak, preferring to die right here, with Taylor's hands kneading his flesh, her legs wrapped around him. But he must have been wrong. Pearl didn't come. He closed his eyes once more and surrendered to Taylor's ministrations.

"Is this helping?" she asked, her mouth so close to his ear that he was sure he felt her warm breath.

"Oh, yeah," he said. "Oh, God, yeah."

"Maybe I should stop. You haven't been very nice to me, you know."

"Don't stop. Please. I'll give you the whole ranch if you'll just promise to keep rubbing me right there."

"The whole ranch, eh?"

He thought about nodding, but that might disturb her hands.

"Tell you what. You can keep your ranch. However, I do want something."

"You mean you're not doing this out of the goodness of your heart?"

"I don't think so." She hesitated for a second. "Nope, I'm not."

"I'm glad we've cleared that up," he said, fighting his smile.

"Me, too." She shifted her hands down so her palms rested on his shoulder blades. Again, the first hint of pressure hurt, then turned into bliss.

"Zach," she said, only she didn't just say his name. She almost sang it, drawing it out into two syllables.

"No," he said, not even bothering to open his eyes.

"But—"

"No," he said.

She stopped his massage.

"Hey!"

"Tell me one reason I should make you feel better?"

"Because you're a wonderful woman. A humanitarian. A credit to your gender."

"And you're full of beans."

"You've accused me of that before. Something tells me that propriety is holding you back from saying something else."

"For a stubborn mule, you're very observant."

He gripped her legs a little harder—not much, but enough to make her aware that he was still there, and wanted more. She picked up on the hint and continued with the massage.

"What if..." she said, leaning closer to him. Close enough for her breasts to touch his back.

He had to wonder if she was doing it on purpose. It wouldn't work. He wasn't going to change his mind. Certainly not just because he could feel her stiff nipples through the thin sheen of her bathing suit.

"What if—" her mouth almost touched his ear "—I come along as the cook's helper. That way, I won't be a distraction to the boys."

"All you'd have to do is be on the same continent to distract the boys," he said.

"Come on, Zach. I promise, I'll be good."

That was the last thing he wanted. She leaned in a bit more, rubbing her soft breasts on his back, making him acutely aware that what he wanted, no *needed*, was for Taylor to be bad. Very bad.

"Please?" she whispered.

"All right," he said. "You can come, but—"

Her hands disappeared from his back, and so did her breasts. Her legs moved so quickly that he lost his grip and slid down under the water. By the time he sputtered to the surface again, Taylor was on the other side of the hot tub.

"Hey!"

"I don't know about you," she said, "but I'm starving."

He watched her climb out, step by step. From this angle, he got a wonderful view of her very enticing back—especially that little glimpse of pale skin that peeked out from the bottom of her bathing suit. Then she was over the side, with her towel circling her body.

Starving? Yes, he was starving. But not for food.

Chapter Nine

Taylor hurried inside the house, afraid that if she didn't, Zach would see her shaking. He might just have thought she was chilly, but Zach was too perceptive. He would probably guess that her condition was a direct result of touching him.

Although her tactic had worked, and she had gotten him to agree to take her on the drive, it had backfired, too. Touching him like that, feeling his hips between her legs, her hands massaging the firm muscles beneath his warm skin, had taken her to a place she didn't want to go. Taken her so fast she'd lost her breath along the way.

The kiss had been bad enough, but this was worse. No matter how she'd tried to tell herself he was just a man, like any other man—and a cowboy to boot—she couldn't seem to get it through her head. Instead, she kept thinking about his kiss. Now the feel of him had been added to the arsenal.

She went into the kitchen expecting to see Pearl, but the room was empty. A tray was set out with two covered plates, a bottle of wine and two glasses. Zach would be coming in any second, and she knew she wasn't going to be able to camouflage her confusion. She needed to get to her room and think rationally about all this.

Moving quickly, she took her plate, some silverware and a soda from the fridge. Just as she turned to make her getaway, Zach walked in.

He had a towel wrapped around his waist. She couldn't tell if he'd left his suit outside or not. God, she hoped not. A naked Zach would be impossible to talk to.

"What's that?" he asked, nodding at the tray.

"Dinner."

"Great. I'm hungry as hell. I'll meet you at the table."

"No!" she said, then realized how desperate she sounded. "Um, I thought I'd just take this up to my room."

He looked at her, his gaze holding her in place, and what she saw there made her wonder if she'd fought so hard to go on the drive because of her article, or because she wanted more time with him. The soda can slipped out of her hand, and she jumped back.

"Are you okay?" he asked, moving toward her. "What's wrong?"

She moved another step back, needing some space between them. "I'm fine. It just slipped."

As he bent down to pick up the can, her gaze went to his back. The bruise was distinct, but not as bad as she'd imagined. Her free hand moved to touch him, but she stopped just shy. He stood up in time to see the blush heat her cheeks.

"I don't think you should open this one," he said. "It's all shook up."

"I know just how it feels," she whispered.

"What?"

"Nothing. I'd better get going. It's late." She stepped to the right, looking for a path around him so they wouldn't touch.

"Don't," he said.

"What?"

"Come eat dinner at the table with me."

She looked down at her bare feet on the cold tile floor. "I don't think so."

He touched her then, on the arm. "We need to talk," he said.

This was it. He knew. Knew that she wanted him. That her insides trembled and grew moist just from looking at his bare chest.

"About the drive."

She let go of a breath she hadn't known she'd been holding. "The drive."

"Yeah. I know I said it was okay for you to go, but I don't think it's such a good idea."

The embarrassment at her libidinous thoughts changed instantly to anger, and all of a sudden his proximity didn't bother her. She put the plate and silverware down on the counter, then turned to him so quickly that her towel slipped off. She stepped over it, and put her hands on her hips. "Now just wait one second," she said. "You can't take it back. No way. You said I can go, and I'm going."

"But—"

"You have yet to give me one legitimate reason for staying behind."

"You want a reason?" he asked. "How's this?" Then his hands grabbed her upper arms and he pulled her roughly to his chest. His lips crushed hers with a kiss that made her gasp. He took advantage of her surprise and thrust his tongue inside, teasing her mouth, stealing her reason. All she could do was cling to his back and succumb. Her eyelids fluttered closed, and she met his tongue with her own. He moaned deeply, and pressed himself up against her.

She felt his desire pressing her belly. She could feel right away that he was naked under the scanty towel, and that with one simple motion that towel could be ripped away and then...

The kiss grew more urgent, and she ran her hands gently down his back. All the way to his waist. She eased her fingers underneath the terry cloth, but then she stilled. No. She couldn't do this. Not in the kitchen. Not with him.

Her riotous thoughts quieted when she felt his hand on her breast. He cupped her, gently squeezing. Not satisfied with that intimacy, he slid his fingers underneath her bathing suit. His hand went to her nipple, already stiff and aching, and he captured the bud between his finger and thumb and rubbed it, lightly, with just enough friction to drive her insane.

He broke the kiss. When she looked up at him, the desire in his eyes made her moan. "Come to my room," he said, his voice low and gravelly.

"I can't," she said, even though everything in her body urged her to go.

"You're so beautiful. When you touched me out there...Taylor, I want you. Please."

The sensation in her nipple made it hard to think. He kept rubbing her, increasing the friction so she thought she might scream. With her last ounce of sanity, she put her hand over his, stopping him. Then she took his wrist and pulled his hand from her suit. "No," she said. "We can't."

"Why not?"

"Because we'd both regret it."

"I wouldn't."

"Maybe not. But I would."

"I see," he said, hurt clouding the fire in his eyes. He stepped back.

His desire hadn't left entirely. She could see the pull on the towel. All she had to do was touch him, say one simple word, and she'd know what it was like to be taken by this man. This hard man with his fierceness just barely below the surface. Making love to him would be unlike anything she'd done before. She knew that with absolute certainty.

And that's why she had to be strong. How could she leave once she'd let him inside? She forced her gaze up. He knew where she'd been looking and he wasn't in the least embarrassed.

"I guess it's too late to say I was kidding," he said.

"I guess."

"I won't hurt you," he said.

"You won't mean to. But you will. I'm leaving soon, Zach. I'm going back to my life. This matters to me. I can't make love and walk away. I'm not built that way."

"I understand." He turned to walk to the sink. He grabbed a glass from the dish drainer and filled it with water. Then he slowly drank it down. When he finished, he put the glass in the sink. "Will you reconsider about the drive?" he said, staring out the window.

"If you insist, I won't come," she said. "But I'd still like to. All I can tell you is that I'll do my best to be inconspicuous. I'll stay with the chuck wagon, if you like. Or do night-hawk work. I won't bother you. I promise."

"You can't help it," he said.

Then he turned, the evidence of his desire gone. Maybe more than that gone.

"All right," he said reluctantly.

"Thank you."

"Don't. It's not going to be easy."

"I know."

He nodded at her, his mouth tight, his brow creased, and then he walked out, leaving his dinner behind. Taylor bent down and picked up her towel, convincing herself she'd done the right thing, despite the hollow ache inside her.

ZACH CURSED LOUDLY as he sat up in bed. His back and shoulder hurt like hell. A good night's sleep would have helped. Unfortunately, he hadn't had one. He'd dreamed of her. Stirred awake by his body's reactions, he'd gotten out of bed twice, only to find that it didn't matter whether he was awake or asleep—either way Taylor tormented him.

He kept telling himself that she was just another woman. Just someone passing briefly through his life. It didn't help. He'd almost convinced himself that he just wanted a woman in a general way, but when he thought of other women he could visit, none of them appealed.

The last time he'd looked at the clock, it had been four-twenty. He must have slept for an hour, because his alarm had awakened him. Now he faced a grueling day, and the pressure wouldn't ease up before they left on the drive. He moved his shoulder and winced. Everything hurt. Even his eyes.

It was all her fault.

He cursed once more, and headed for his shower.

By the time he'd finished dressing and headed to breakfast, he'd made up his mind to ignore her—to just pretend she wasn't there. He'd ask Charlie to help her pick her string, and he'd ask Stu, the wagon cook, to show her her responsibilities on the drive.

With any luck, he wouldn't run into her at all. Ex-

cept for meals, of course. At least there, the boys and
Pearl would keep her occupied.

He walked into the dining room. Most of the men
were already there, and so was Taylor. She sat next to
Cal, and the two of them were deep in conversation.
Zach frowned, moving over to his seat.

Taylor never looked up. She just kept on talking.
He saw her smile, too. When she laughed, he coughed,
but even that didn't make her look at him.

He filled his plate and began to eat. Charlie said
something to him, but when he looked up, the foreman
just shook his head and said, "Never mind." Which
was fine with him. He was in no mood for chitchat.
Unlike some people.

TAYLOR LISTENED to Stu go over the menus for the
five-day drive as she watched Johnny Haslip, one of
the younger boys, trying to rope a fence post. The boy
wasn't having a lot of luck, but his persistence im-
pressed her. She could see from here some of what he
was doing wrong. For one thing, he was gripping the
rope too tightly, which caused it to wind up and kink.
He needed to have a very light touch, which was a
hard thing to learn.

One of the older boys—she thought his name was
Little Danny—rode by the fence and laughed at
Johnny's latest miss. Taylor frowned.

"Don't worry about him," Stu said. "Zach's gonna
help him out. He promised to teach the boy to rope
before the drive."

"The drive isn't that far off."

"Yeah, but I still wouldn't worry about it. Now, I mostly use corn oil these days…"

Taylor turned her back on Johnny to pay attention to cooking class, but she couldn't help thinking that she ought to go talk to him. Warn him not to expect too much. Zach may have promised to help the boy, but she'd bet money he'd forgotten. She certainly hadn't heard Zach mention it. But for all she knew, Johnny wasn't expecting help. He was about seventeen or eighteen. Plenty of time to learn that counting on a cowboy was like whistling in the wind. It just didn't go anywhere.

She wasn't a great roper, but she knew a thing or two. Once she finished with Stu, and then Charlie, she'd find Johnny and she'd give him a hand.

ZACH SKIPPED DINNER. He was tired as all get out, and hungry, too, but he didn't want to stop. Another hour of work, and he could grab something to eat and then go right to bed.

He'd spent the day going over equipment, checking all the saddles, the bedrolls, the ropes and the chuck wagon. All he had left to do tonight was to go over the medical equipment, pack the tent he was bringing for Taylor, and do a final check of each of the horses. Over the next couple of days, he'd spend time with the boys who hadn't been on a drive before. Make sure they knew what they were expected to do.

He pulled the medical kit from the chuck wagon,

and the first thing he did was find the aspirin bottle. He opened it and took four pills, hoping it would be enough to ease the pain in his back and shoulder. If he could sleep tonight, by tomorrow the worst of it should be over. And he was so dog-tired right now that, Taylor or no Taylor, he was going to sleep.

It only took ten minutes to give the medical kit his stamp of approval, and a few minutes more to pack the tent. He headed toward the corral, but first he looked back at the house. He could see inside the living room, but not to the dining room. Did she wonder where he was?

He shook off his thoughts and began his last chore. All he was doing was checking to make sure none of the horses were injured or had thrown a shoe. He was ninety-percent sure they were all in good shape. But he wouldn't go to sleep until he was one-hundred-percent sure.

TAYLOR FELT the buzz of excitement all around the dinner table. Tomorrow they would ride, driving the herd to the high pasture. It felt like Christmas Eve.

She smiled at Cal. She had to give Frankie credit. Cal was really a nice guy. Polite, intelligent, clean. He even had a good sense of humor. The only thing wrong with him was that he was determined to be a cowboy for the rest of his life. To follow in his hero's footsteps. He worshipped at the altar of Zach, and there was nothing to be done about that. If Frankie ended up marrying Cal, they'd live here in Wyoming, although, knowing Zach, not on the ranch. Cal wanted to work for Zach until he'd made enough money to get his own spread. But that, too, would be here.

She turned to her dessert—an unbelievably delicious cherry cobbler—and let the excited conversation of the ranch hands wash over her. The boys were psyched. For most of them, it was their first drive, and she could tell that their expectations were more dramatic than the reality would be. A lot more.

Mostly, working wild cattle was tiring, hot, dirty and grueling. The day lasted as long as the sunlight, and the nights were spent on cold, hard ground. The food was probably good—Stu certainly took pride in his work—but it wasn't going to be a banquet.

They did have a few wonderful things in store. The camaraderie of cowboys on a drive was intense. They all looked out for each other, and they had to work as a team in order to keep the herd in check. If they were lucky, they'd come back with lifelong friends, and a real sense of accomplishment.

Zach was giving them a gift, she had to admit that. Over the past few days, she'd heard their stories. What they'd been like before Zach had taken them in. Mostly they'd been alone. Whether from neglect, or bad luck, not one of them had a family they could count on. They'd all found Zach through friends or friends-of-friends. No agency was involved. No court. Someone from town or a nearby ranch would call Zach and tell him about a young man. Before long, Zach would find that young man and offer him a job. A place to stay. A place to start again. Of course, not all of them accepted. There were rules to be followed— strict ones. But those who came tended to do well. Zach pulled the reins tight, but he was fair. The end result was a group of good kids, each with a fine future ahead of him. Which kind of spoiled the thrust of Taylor's article.

She'd stayed up late the night before, working on her computer. Her original outline had to be tossed out the window. Not that the heart of it wasn't intact. She hadn't changed her mind about that. Cowboys were still bad news to women. While Zach was teaching them about cattle and horses, he was also teaching them that women had no place in their world. That was the bottom line: women and cowboys don't mix. They never would.

She glanced again at his empty seat. Charlie had told her Zach wouldn't come in until he was absolutely sure everything was ready for tomorrow. She understood. The guy hadn't stopped all week. His back must hurt, but he didn't let that slow him down. From the way he looked on the few occasions she'd run into him, he hadn't been sleeping all that well, either. He must be dead on his feet.

"Taylor?"

She turned to Pearl, who'd taken the seat next to her. "I'm sorry. Yes?"

"You haven't said much tonight. You okay?"

She nodded. "Just a little tired."

"Has he been working you too hard?"

Taylor smiled. "No," she said. "I was up too late last night. Writing the article."

Pearl nodded. "I'm certainly looking forward to reading it. Do you have everything you need for tomorrow?"

"I think so."

Pearl turned to the table, watching as each of the boys cleared their plates. She smiled at the laughter and the good-natured teasing. "He's stubborn because he cares so much," she said.

Taylor knew she was talking about Zach. "I know. But that doesn't make him right."

"About the girls?"

Taylor nodded.

"Maybe not. But he hasn't had a lot of luck with women. Starting from his mother on."

Taylor didn't say anything, hoping Pearl would go on. The silence built for a long moment, then Pearl turned back to her.

"His mother left when he was eight months old."

"Left?"

Pearl nodded. "She'd gotten pregnant, and then she married Zach's father. The woman hated the ranch. She wanted nothing to do with it. Zach's daddy, my brother, tried to make it as nice as he could for her, but it didn't work. One night, she just disappeared. Someone said they thought she went out to California, but who knows? She never contacted any of us again."

"That's terrible."

"Yeah. But my brother raised Zach to be a fine man. I like to think I helped."

"So you moved here after she left?"

"Yep. Never regretted it, either. I've had a very good life."

"He's lucky he had you."

"Yeah, he is." She smiled. "I tried to tell him that not all women are like his mother, but I don't think he believes me. Especially not after what happened with Belinda."

"Belinda?"

"She was from Texas, too. San Antonio. A real pretty thing. But she wasn't a good person. She hurt Zach. Not just because he fell for her and she left him, but because she played him for a fool. She was a regular con artist. She got money—a bundle—but even more. She stole his belief that he could find someone nice and settle down. She helped him think he had bad luck with women. Then there was a string of accidents. Most of them not serious, except that one... Since then, he's never had another girlfriend. Not for long, anyway. Which is a real shame. Of all the men I know, I think Zach would make the best father. He's a father to these boys, in a way."

Pearl leaned in a little closer and took Taylor's hand in hers. "The thing is, he made a decision when he was too young to know better, and he hasn't opened up his heart enough to see that the decision was hasty. It's a pity. And a waste."

"What happened to Zach's father?"

"He passed away eight years ago."

"He never remarried?"

"No. He never did. He never even entertained the idea. I think Zach learned a little too much from that example."

Taylor squeezed Pearl's hand. She understood Zach better now. How he'd come to be the man he was. But she couldn't agree totally with Pearl. Taylor had made some of her own decisions when she was young—wise decisions. And then she'd gone against her better judgment and fallen for a cowboy. All that had done was prove to her that she'd been a fool.

Zach knew what was right for him. Just like she knew what was right for her.

"Well," Pearl said, "I'd better get started on the dishes. You get a good night's sleep, you hear? You're going to need it. I'll see you in the morning."

Taylor nodded. She got up from the table, but she didn't go right up to bed. Instead, she headed out for a walk. She wanted to be alone. To think.

The night air felt good on her skin. She took a deep breath and let it out slowly. Her thoughts turned to Zach, and what Pearl had said. Knowing what he'd gone through made her feel a little closer to him. Their situations hadn't been all that different. He'd been without a mother, and she, for all intents and purposes, had been without a father. Which made her even more determined to keep her distance from him. They were completely wrong for each other. She needed someone who'd put her first. Zach needed a woman who'd be satisfied with seconds.

She walked toward the barn, listening to the quiet. As she passed the great door, she saw some lights out by the corral. Curious, she headed that way. There, in the light from a pickup truck, Zach stood next to Johnny, coaching the boy as he twirled his rope.

She watched for a long time. Zach was patient. Although she couldn't hear him, she could see the kindness in his touch. Johnny had roped the fence post four times when she finally turned back toward the house, more confused than ever.

Chapter Ten

Zach looked at his watch. The drive had finally begun, and only about a half hour late. Not bad when he considered how many tenderfoots he had working for him.

Charlie was up ahead, leading them to the huge holding pen where most of the cattle had been for the past few months. They'd be herded up to the high pasture to graze for the spring, and then there would be the roundup, during which they'd be brought down again and readied for market.

This drive was good training for his boys. They'd pick up wild cattle along the way, and once they reached the high pasture, the cows would have to be inoculated. It wasn't as hard on a cowboy as roundup, and it would let Zach see how the boys were developing.

But on this drive, he'd have to keep especially alert. This time, they were traveling with Taylor.

She'd kept out of his way the last couple of days. They'd eaten together, of course, and he'd seen her working in the barn, and with Stu. But they hadn't talked much. That didn't mean he hadn't thought about her. Or dreamed about her. Or wanted her.

He'd almost changed his mind a hundred times about letting her come. But in the end, he hadn't stopped her. He wasn't sure why. Most likely because he was a damn fool.

He urged Falcon on as soon as the last boy had passed him. Taylor rode between Cal and Carlos, the night hawk. Carlos was probably telling her what it was like to be the night man in charge of the horses. Filling her in on what she'd have to look out for when it was her turn to spell him.

Helping the cook and spelling the night hawk should be enough to keep her out of trouble. But he doubted any job would make things completely safe. The boys were too aware of her.

He'd seen them watching her. Smiling. Trying to get her attention. He'd been sharp with Little Danny and Pete when they'd had their eyes on Taylor's backside instead of saddling their horses. They'd moaned when he told them to do the job again, but, sure enough, Pete hadn't cinched his saddle properly. They hadn't even left, and the boys were already letting her get to them.

His gaze traveled up the line once more. Everyone was in good spirits, and a few of the boys were singing one of the songs Pearl had taught them. Singing around cattle, as long as the songs were on the quiet side, helped soothe the animals, and he'd even seen it stop a stampede. A couple of the boys had really good voices, but Jim, the rough string rider, was stone-cold tone deaf. Zach just hoped the cows didn't notice.

Jesse, whom he hadn't seen since breakfast, moved his horse next to Falcon. "Hey boss."

"Yeah?"

"Johnny said that you're helping him get ready for the rodeo."

"That's right."

"I was wondering…"

"Yeah?"

"I was just thinking that I might…you know—I'd like to do that."

"Do what?"

"Be in the rodeo."

"I don't see why that would be a problem."

"Great." The boy smiled broadly. "See, I was thinking about barrel racing. I think I'd be pretty good at that. I've practiced a little, on my own."

"That wasn't ever my best event, but I think I can help you out."

"Oh, you don't need to. Taylor said she would. She's won at rodeos all over the southwest."

"She has?"

"Yeah. So maybe you could tell me how to sign up. You know, enter."

"Sure."

"Thanks, boss!" Jesse spurred his horse forward and rode up next to Taylor.

Zach heard her laugh. He scowled. Trouble. The

woman was nothing but trouble. He never should have let her come along.

TAYLOR WAS AMAZED at the size of the herd. Hereford cattle milled for more than a mile to the east. Mostly mature cattle, but enough calves to see that the herd was healthy and growing. Taking these animals to the high pasture was going to be one big job. But from what she'd learned in her talks with the boys, they were ready to tackle it.

To a man, they'd all sung Zach's praises. Talked about him as if he were not just a cowboy, but *the* cowboy. They all wanted to be like him. And they all desperately wanted his approval.

It made sense. He was the only man in charge in a closed environment. But she couldn't help wondering what potential was being lost by keeping the boys on the ranch, and not exposing them to other walks of life. When she'd brought up the idea of investigating other careers, they'd all looked at her as if she were nuts. She'd thought she'd made some headway with two of the boys when she mentioned college, but they told her they were going to study animal husbandry, then come right back to the ranch life.

In their minds, that life was still romantic and glamorous. An honorable and worthy endeavor. It wasn't just a fantasy that captured young girl's fancies. The mythology ran deep and wide through America. She could see that her article was more important than she'd ever imagined.

Of course, she wasn't going to change everyone's mind. That wasn't possible. But maybe one or two young people would think twice before making a decision that would affect them the rest of their lives. Her main concern was Frankie, though. Now that she'd spent some time with Cal, she could understand Frankie's love for him. He was a sweet, decent guy, and he loved Frankie something awful.

But there was no way he could convince Taylor that the life he had chosen was the right life for her sister. Frankie could be so much more than a ranch wife. She *should* be more. She was bright, beautiful, witty, strong. The world was her oyster, and not a prairie oyster at that. Frankie should be going to college, taking all kinds of classes to expose herself to what was available. Instead, she had closed down, and all she wanted was to live the kind of life that had made their mother old before her time.

It was no life for a vibrant woman. Although when Taylor was a kid, she'd thought there was nothing in the world that could be better than being a cowgirl.

The drive today had made her remember. Gosh, the boys were so excited. Everything about the morning had been tinged with electricity. Breakfast had been eaten with uncommon gusto, and all the boys had lined up to give Pearl big thank-you kisses on the cheek. Of course, Pearl had loved every second of it. She'd also slipped each of them a little surprise package to be opened up tonight by the campfire. No one peeked inside the bundles, but the luscious rich smell of chocolate couldn't be hidden by the wrapping.

Even Zach had been caught up in the festive atmosphere, although he tried like hell not to show it. But she was getting to know him a little. She knew that his gruff demeanor only slightly disguised his excitement. Although she'd only seen him briefly, she'd thought about him constantly. Not just while she was working on the article, but when she rode, and when she worked in the barn. The nights were the worst though. The dreams. Full of heat and passion that left her gasping for breath in her queen-size bed.

Now that they were finally on the drive, she'd have much more important things to occupy her mind.

She turned her gaze toward him and saw him wince as he moved his shoulder. It was still sore. She'd brought plenty of liniment and aspirin, and right then she decided that she would massage him tonight. It wasn't a very smart thing to do—she remembered far too clearly what touching him so intimately had done to her—but she couldn't let him suffer. Not when he had to work so hard.

"Hey Taylor!"

She turned on her saddle and saw Eddie and Eric—the two boys she'd spent the least amount of time with—waving at her. She smiled and waved back.

"Watch this," Eric yelled, swinging his rope in a big circle above his head. He leaned forward and tossed the lasso, but it only hit the back of a cow, then trailed to the ground.

Eric's curse made her eyes pop. It wasn't exactly the kind of talk she expected from someone as sweet-looking as Eric. Before she could respond, Zach rode up to the boy and started giving him what-for.

Taylor couldn't hear the words, but she could guess at them. Especially when she watched Eric's face grow pale. Guaranteed, she wouldn't be hearing that partic-ular epithet for the rest of the drive.

Zach left a chastened-looking Eric to ride up next to her. It took him a while to get through the cattle, but he did. "Sorry about that," he said, in a surpris-ingly low tone.

"That's okay."

"Shh. We need to keep it quiet while the cattle get used to us. I was just explaining that to Eric."

"I'll bet," she said, speaking in a stage whisper.

"Next time one of the boys wants to show off for you, I'd appreciate it if you'd play it down. There aren't any emergency rooms out where we're headed, and no one wants to see anyone get hurt."

"I didn't know he was going to try that rope trick," she said.

"All the same. Just don't get too exuberant."

"Exuberant?" she repeated, her voice rising.

He put his hand out to quiet her. "Yes. Exuberant. It means—"

"I know what it means," she said. "Although I'm shocked that *you* do."

"Right," he said, barely moving his lips. Falcon started getting a little jumpy, which made Paladin jerk his head and snort. "I'm just a dumb old cowboy. Stupid as a fence post."

"I never said that."

"You didn't have to. Your attitude said it all."

"My attitude? I think you're forgetting who the stubborn mule has been this whole week."

She turned her attention to her horse. Paladin was really shaky. Then Taylor noticed that the air had changed. Something was wrong. The cattle were tensing, and they were starting to circle, which wasn't a good thing.

"Zach, the cows."

"Just stay calm," he said, his voice low and easy. He turned his head toward Jesse, Cal and Pete. "What's that song Pearl taught you boys?"

Jesse began the song, haltingly at first. Then Cal and Pete picked up the tune. It was just an old folk song, one she hadn't heard since childhood, but it sounded sweet right then. The other boys joined in, and soon enough she saw the cattle slow down. They quieted too, as if they'd been anxious to hear their favorite melody.

She also saw that the singing had another potent effect. None of the boys looked nervous anymore. They were too busy singing—keeping their voices soft as they'd been taught—to be scared about the potential stampede.

"It's working," she said to Zach.

"I know. Just keep steady with me. We're going to start to move the cattle out before they catch on."

"I didn't mean it was working on the cattle," she whispered. "Although I see it is. What I meant was, it's working with the boys."

He looked at her with that half smile on his face. "Yeah. It is."

"You didn't think I'd notice?"

He shrugged. "No reason for you to."

"Zach, I'm trying to give you a compliment. It's a very smart thing you did here."

His grin changed so it wasn't crooked anymore. "Thanks, I—" Then he seemed to remember that he was supposed to be angry with her. "Yeah, well…"

She shook her head. "It's no use, Zach. I'm gonna be here for the duration. You might as well just accept it."

He snorted.

She tried to keep a straight face. Then something hit her. The boys had gone on to another song, and it wasn't a folk song. She glanced around, and saw that they were all looking at Zach and her. The two of them were smack dab in the middle of hundreds of cows. Right next to each other. Leaning in, so they could speak at a whisper.

No wonder the boys had changed their tune.

She laughed, quietly, as they began the second verse of "Feelings."

ZACH ENDED UP riding behind Taylor the whole day. At first, the boys kept away from her, but as the day went on, and especially after lunch, they all seemed to find one excuse or another to talk to her. Not that she minded. She was so happy that her smile looked like it might rust in place.

At least nothing bad had happened, with the exception of Charlie reminding him of their wager. It hadn't been easy handing over a hundred dollars of his hard-earned cash. But a bet was a bet.

Of course, it was only the first day. The way Taylor was distracting the boys from watching the herd wasn't good, though. Not good at all.

He'd have a talk with his crew tonight. Another hour, and they'd start getting ready for the night. They had to build a corral for the horses, set up the chuck wagon, put out their bedrolls, build a couple of fires, and then post sentries to the herd. All that before the sun went down. But Zach was looking forward to it. The activity would keep everyone busy. Even Taylor.

She was talking to Stu now, more than likely planning dinner. Stu had been cooking for Zach for the last seven years. He was a good man, but he liked things done his way. He'd never wanted help—until now. It made Zach think of Paladin. How Taylor had tamed that horse in nothing flat. It seemed that her magic worked on more than horses. She certainly had charmed his boys.

Hell, she'd charmed him. He didn't like the way he kept thinking about her. Obsessing about her. It was bad enough that any woman had infiltrated his territory, but Taylor—she was more than just any woman. She was a fine cowhand. A good, strong worker. She could rope, she could ride, and she didn't complain about any of it. What was worse, she looked so beautiful doing it all. Her dark hair all shiny, her lips so pink and moist. That T-shirt of hers stretched over her breasts and tucked so neatly into her tight jeans. It was enough to drive a saint to sin—and he was no saint.

Ever since he'd kissed her, since he'd felt that lush flesh beneath his palm, he'd been thinking about doing it again. He'd shake off the thoughts, but as soon as he let his guard down, they came back. Even the drive and all the responsibility it entailed wasn't enough to keep his mind on business.

"What are you thinking about?"

He turned sharply. Taylor had slowed Paladin, and now she was right next to him. He'd been so busy thinking about her that he hadn't even noticed. "Nothing," he said, turning his gaze back to the herd.

"That was some expression for thinking about nothing."

"What do you mean?"

"If I had to guess, I'd say you were picturing a nice, juicy steak, or a big slice of chocolate cake, because honey, I've never seen anyone look quite that hungry."

He coughed. "You caught me," he said. "I guess I'm looking forward to dinner."

She held out the packet of cake Pearl had given her. "Here," she said. "You can have this. I only nibbled on it a little."

"Thanks," he said, shaking his head. "I can wait.

We'll be setting up camp in a bit. Dinner won't be long after that.''

"Okay, but don't say I never offered. Some people in my family would be shocked to hear I was willing to part with chocolate.''

"You like that, eh?''

She sighed, loudly, he thought, because he heard it over the constant shuffle of hooves and all the other noises that accompanied a mass migration like this.

"Sometimes it's worse than others,'' she said. "When it's really bad, no one is safe.''

"I had a barn cat like that once. Only, he liked cantaloupe, if you can believe it. He'd have fought off a mountain lion over a slice of melon. Never seen anything like it before or since.''

"I can understand an animal like that,'' she said. "Fierce. Undeterred. He was probably a heck of a mouser, right?''

"Right you are.''

"Well, heck. Now you've got *me* hungry.''

"For mice?''

She laughed. "No, but I take back my generous offer of cake.''

"Don't worry about it. I'm not much of a chocolate fan.'' He watched her take a little piece of cake and pop it in her mouth. The sight was unimaginably erotic to him. Her lips, the way her eyes half closed and then the tip of her pink tongue took that tiny lick. He grew uncomfortable on the saddle, and shifting didn't help.

The best idea was to simply ignore her, but he couldn't.

She swallowed and turned to smile at him, but after one glimpse of his face, her grin faltered. She tilted her head, looking at him with a question in her eyes. "What's that?" she asked.

"What's what?"

"The way you're looking at me."

He quickly glanced away. "I wasn't looking at you in any particular way."

"Yes, you were. I saw you."

"Must have been a trick of the light."

"My, my," she said, slowly, drawing the two words out.

He turned to her again. "What?"

"Nothing," she said, her smile now firmly in place. A very cocky smile.

"I told you, I wasn't looking at you."

"I know."

"So, what's that grin for?"

"Grin? What grin?"

He wanted to do something. Preferably with his hands around her throat. "Women," he said.

"That's right, Zach." Her eyes narrowed in triumph. "No matter how you try to act like you don't like us, you can't help it. Face it, big guy. It's basic biology. And it's a hell of a lot stronger than you'd like it to be."

"You're crazy."

"Am I?"

He nodded. "You think I want you just because you're a woman? That I can't help myself, right?"

"Yep."

"Wrong, sweetheart." He leaned over to her, and put his mouth right next to her ear. "I want you because I know what you taste like. I know what you feel like under that blouse of yours. And I know that you want it just as badly as I do."

Chapter Eleven

Taylor thought about what Zach had said, as she helped Stu with dinner. Which didn't turn out to be a good thing for the dinner. She spilled two cups of flour, doubled the salt in the corn, and forgot to take the biscuits out of the oven until they were blackened on the bottom. She swore to Stu that it was just nerves, and she'd be a better helper in the future, but she could tell he didn't believe her.

The boys were a lot more forgiving. They were all tired, but so ravenous she could have fed them almost anything and they would have been grateful.

And yet none of their boisterous good humor, or their excited discussions about the first day of the drive were sufficient to keep her mind from wandering back to Zach.

He wanted her. She'd known that, of course, especially after they'd kissed in the kitchen. But she hadn't understood until tonight that he wanted *her*. That it was personal. Not vaguely hormonal, or because there weren't any other women on the ranch. Hearing him was convincing, but seeing his eyes, his face, she finally had understood that she had a problem on her hands.

Because as he'd spoken those charged words, her whole body had reacted as if she'd been struck by lightning.

He'd said she wanted him just as badly as he wanted her. And as much as she'd tried to deny it, as much as she'd like it to be untrue, it was no use. Three hours had gone by and her nipples were still erect. She'd had to put an apron on, just so the whole gang wouldn't see her embarrassing state. That wasn't the only physical reaction she'd had trouble with, but it was the most obvious. The others—a blush that wouldn't die, a need to squeeze her legs together, the rapid beating of her heart—were all more subtle, yet much more annoying. Mostly because she just knew that Zach was on to her.

He'd been a cool customer, never letting the boys see him ruffled, but he'd let *her* know. Once, while she was standing at the stove, he'd brushed up against her back. Instead of quickly moving on, he'd lingered, his chest, his waist, his hips just touching her. She'd felt his hot breath on her neck. When she looked down, she noticed her hands trembling.

Later, when she'd prepared his dinner plate, he'd leaned over and brushed a hair from her cheek. The feel of his callused thumb was enough to freeze her in place. He held her captive with his gaze, with his touch, until he decided she'd had enough. Then he moved his hand, and the spell was broken.

Now he sat in the big circle of cowboys, eating, listening, glancing back at her from time to time. Waiting for her to join them, to sit in the space he'd saved for her. She got her dinner plate and headed for him, determined not to let him fluster her any further.

That lasted about one hot second.

He'd looked up at her. That's all. Just a look, and that quick, crooked grin. She barely made it to the ground without spilling her meal all over him.

"Taylor, did you see?"

She looked over at Pete, normally too dark and somber for a seventeen-year-old. There was nothing somber about him now, though. His whole face lit up with excitement. He'd barely touched his food.

"Did I see what?"

"When I roped that calf! It was just like Zach said. All I had to do was relax, and let the rope do the work. I got that sucker the first try."

"No, I'm sorry I missed it," Taylor said. "You'll have to do it again so I can see."

"Yeah. Okay. Man, though, I wish you'd been there."

"You find me tomorrow morning, okay?"

Pete nodded, then tackled his chili.

"What about me?" Johnny asked. "I can do it, too."

She looked at his eager face, then at the other boys sitting in the big circle, cross-legged, with their plates balanced precariously on bony knees. The energy simply poured off them in waves, undeterred by discomfort, the smell of way too many cattle doing what cattle do, and the exhaustion from working such a long day. Each one of them looked as if they were ready to climb right back in the saddle. She knew, too, that if Zach asked them to, they would keep going until they dropped.

They wanted her to applaud their victories, but they wanted Zach to be proud of them. Although each of the boys was an individual with all the differences that entailed, there was something markedly similar about them—they all wanted to be like Zach.

She felt sure none of them realized how they aped his stance, how they wore their hats just the way he did. Or that when he ate, they ate. When he stopped, most of them stopped, too.

She couldn't—wouldn't—deny it. He'd done something fine with these young men. If only he could have shown them more than the narrow life on the ranch.

"You know what I'd like to hear," she said, putting her plate down in front of her. "I'd like to hear how you all came to be on this cattle drive." She turned to Johnny first. "You start."

Johnny looked at Zach as if waiting for permission. When Zach nodded, Johnny turned his attention to Taylor. "I'd gotten in some trouble. We—me and Eddie and Eric—we borrowed this car—" his gaze crept to Zach again, and then he looked at his hands "—we stole this car. It was my second offense, and the judge was gonna send me to a juvenile prison. Only Zach said I could come here.''

''Me, too,'' piped up Eric, whom she'd only spoken to a couple of times before. ''And same thing for Eddie and Jesse and Pete. Although I don't know if Jesse and Pete stole a car or not.''

''I didn't,'' Jesse said. ''I was in trouble for skipping school. But I hated it. I'm much happier here.''

''What about your education?'' she asked.

''I go to school,'' he said. ''Zach said we all have to get our degrees. But it's not a big high school like I used to go to. Zach, he can tell you about it. He built it.''

She turned to Zach. ''Really?''

He nodded. ''It made sense. I know how important an education is, but I also know it's equally important to have a trade.''

''So you provide both?''

''I'm not the only one. Three other ranchers in the valley do the same. Together we pay for the school and the teachers.''

''That's wonderful,'' she said, meaning it. There, he'd done it again. Surprised her. Made her question herself. He was a different breed of cowboy. Not like the men she'd grown up around. If someone had suggested starting a school for cowboys around her father, he'd have laughed himself hoarse. The only education he'd felt was important was how to take care of a horse, a cow, a gun and a saddle. Anything else was a waste. Unless you were a girl. Then you also needed to know how to cook, clean and sew. And have babies.

Zach was something completely different, which bothered her a lot. He confused her, and made her question things she didn't want to question.

She understood that the boys who worked for him worshiped Zach. But the more she got to know him, the more she saw that he'd earned his hero status. What would have become of these young men if they hadn't had Zach to turn to?

"Would you like some more chili?"

She looked up to see Zach standing in front of her, holding out his hand for her plate. "No, thanks. I'm fine."

"You didn't eat much. This is hard work. Not a good time to be on a diet."

She smiled. "I'm not on a diet. If I was, you'd know it."

"How?"

"I wouldn't be this charming and affable person you see in front of you," she said. "I get a little grouchy when I'm denied dessert."

"A *little* grouchy?"

"Uh-huh."

"I've seen you a little grouchy. And it wasn't because you didn't get your chocolate."

"Me? Never. I've been sweet as pie since I got here."

He shook his head. "You've been a pain in the rear since you got here," he said, and then he leaned down so he was very close to her, and only she could hear him. "A very beautiful pain."

"Stop, you're making me blush."

He shook his head. "No. I know how to make you blush. This isn't it."

Acting as if this little tête-à-tête was nothing more than friendly banter, she handed him her plate, hoping he didn't notice the quiver. She didn't want him to know what his teasing did to her, although she couldn't be at all certain that she was hiding a thing. He looked at her with eyes too knowing. As if he could read her like an open book.

Zach stood up. "After you finish helping Stu with the cleanup, we'll get your tent ready."

"Tent? What tent?"

"I brought one along. You'll be more comfortable that way."

She scrambled to her feet. "I don't want any special treatment," she said. "I can sleep under the stars, just like all the others."

"No," he said, walking toward the chuck wagon.

"Wait a minute. Don't just walk away like that." She caught up to him and reached out to grab his arm. But when she touched him, she pulled back immediately. Touching him made her too shaky. "I don't want to sleep in a tent," she said.

"It's not negotiable."

"Says who?"

"Says me. And this is my playground."

She wanted to strangle him. One moment he was

making her tremble with desire, and the next moment he made her furious. She had the feeling that the anger was the safer of the two emotions.

"Look," he said, turning to face her. "Do you realize what it's like to have a woman like you around? I've got a whole team of kids who have more hormones than brains. They're excited, they're overtired. They don't need the added stimulation of sleeping next to a beautiful woman."

She tried to stoke her anger, but with an argument like that, it wasn't easy. "Oh, well..."

"It's not bad. You'll have enough room for your bed and your other stuff."

"I still think there's something inherently wrong with your logic, but okay."

"I'm glad you approve," he said, fighting a smile.

"I don't. At least I don't think so. Today has been pretty confusing."

"Why?"

She shouldn't tell him. It would just give him more ammunition. He was the enemy, and it wasn't wise to forget that. He was everything that she was against in a man, only some of her black-and-whites were turning into grays. "How come I never met a man like you when I was growing up?" she asked.

"I don't know. What kind of a man am I?"

"Stubborn," she said. "But that's one of the only traits I can connect back to the cowboys I grew up around."

"And?"

He put the plates down, then leaned against the

chuck wagon, crossing his arms over his chest. His hat was pushed forward so it shadowed his eyes. A stubble darkened his chin. He was maybe the best-looking man she'd ever seen. She remembered his kiss, the way he'd stolen her breath, and for a crazy moment she thought of kissing him again. Of touching him, and feeling him touch her. As her cheeks heated, she focused on the wood right next to his left ear. "The men I knew when I was growing up weren't interested in helping anyone. Matter of fact, they had a tendency to get the young men in trouble. Sort of a badge of honor."

"What do you mean, trouble?"

"I mean like getting drunk and busting up the bar. Or taking a fifteen-year-old boy to a hooker as a present. They certainly didn't want to mold them into anything but replicas of themselves. Uneducated, selfish and sometimes just downright mean."

His brow furrowed and he leaned toward her. "So they were all jerks? Every one?"

"Pretty much. Of course I didn't get to know all of them. By the time I was old enough to realize the score, I looked for other interests."

"What about that fiancé of yours? Was he like that?"

She hesitated. But then she decided to face Zach and tell him the truth. "I thought Ben was different. I was wrong."

"How?"

"When I first met him, I thought he was everything wonderful. Handsome—God, but he was handsome.

And he could talk, too. He'd actually been to two years of college, and his repertoire was considerably greater than pickup trucks, guns, horses and cows. We talked about a lot of things that mattered to me. He wasn't much of a reader, so we didn't have that, but he listened really well.''

"So far he sounds like a good man."

"In some ways, he was. But when it came down to choosing his cowboy buddies or me, I never stood a chance. He canceled on me time and time again, because some cowboy or another needed him to help with the cattle, or for a roundup, or just to go drinking. Finally, he told me he'd decided to go out on the rodeo circuit instead of settling down like we'd planned. That was that.''

"I see," Zach said. "So what you're telling me is that this guy, this Ben, was a jackass."

She grinned. "That's what I like about you, Zach. You get right to the point." Her grin faltered a bit as she studied him. It was a little sobering to realize how different Zach was from Ben. "Tell me something. If there was a woman in your life, someone you loved, would you give up your cattle drives? Would any woman ever be able to compete with your ranch?"

"Why would it need to be a competition?"

"Because some women don't like to stay home and wait every night. Some women actually like to spend time with their husbands. They want to raise a family. They want a father for their children, and not just an occasional dirty visitor."

"So you want a man who's home every night, is

that it? Someone who works in an office. Some middle-manager who likes to wash his car on Sunday, and go to the movies on Friday night?''

"What's wrong with that?"

"Not a thing."

"Okay, then," she said. But it wasn't really. Somehow she felt as though she'd just lost an argument. What she didn't understand was how.

"Looks like the boys are getting restless," Zach said, pushing himself off the wagon. "I'd better go set them to work."

She nodded, still unsettled.

Zach took three steps, then stopped. "If I loved a woman," he said carefully, "I'd give up a lot of things. If I had to, even the ranch. But if a woman loved me, she wouldn't ask."

TAYLOR FINISHED putting the last pot away, making sure that everything she'd stowed in the chuck wagon was tightly packed so nothing would come loose on the trail tomorrow. It had taken just over an hour to get everything clean and put away, and to sort out the supplies they'd need to fix breakfast tomorrow. The whole time, she'd thought of only one thing. One man. Embarrassingly enough, all her thoughts had been wicked. She wished she'd never seen him without his shirt on. It made it too easy to picture herself in his arms.

She remembered massaging him in the hot tub, and then it occurred to her that there was no tub out here, hot or otherwise. The best she'd get was a hurried sponge bath with tepid water. From what she knew about cattle drives, she was probably the only one concerned with bathing. One of the most durable memories from her childhood was the smell of the cowboys when they came back from a drive. God, the house reeked. It had taken days for her mother to air everything out. Her father had just laughed. For some unknown reason, coming back smelling like skunks had been something they'd been proud of. If Zach wanted to carry on that tradition, he was in for a fight.

She went toward the campfire, and the big circle of boys who seemed to shimmer in the orange light.

"There she is," Little Danny said. "Hey, Taylor. Is it true you used to be a barrel racer?"

She nodded. "Yep. Won about six blue ribbons in the junior division." Zach wasn't in the circle, and she debated going off to find him, but she didn't really have a reason to. So she sat in between Cal and Jesse.

"Why'd you quit?" Danny asked.

"It was time to explore other things. I got involved in school, and I found a whole world away from the ranch."

"Like sewing and stuff?" Pete asked.

"Like writing. Reading. Music and drama."

"Reading?" Jesse said. "You think reading is better than winning a blue at a rodeo?"

"It can be just as stimulating, yes," she said.

"Maybe for a girl."

"Not just for a girl. For anyone. You might want to give it a try sometime."

"Yeah, right," Jesse said.

"Have you ever heard of Boo Radley?" she asked.

"Boo who?" said Pete, and everyone cracked up.

When they were finished laughing, she tried again. "Boo Radley. And Atticus Finch. Scout and Jem and the night they almost got killed walking home from the Halloween party? No? Oh, my."

"So?" Jesse said. "You gonna tell us or what?"

"Okay," she said. "But first, I think we need some hot chocolate. You shouldn't ever hear about Boo Radley for the first time without something hot and sweet to hold on to."

ZACH STOPPED just outside the circle. He'd intended to tell Taylor that her tent was set up, and that she could go get ready for bed, but it was clear she was busy. The circle had tightened since dinner. The boys were quiet, watching Taylor carefully, listening as if she were telling them the best story ever told. It reminded him of *Peter Pan*, and the lost boys begging Wendy for a bedtime story. In a way, that's just what it was. Not one of these boys had grown up in a decent home, or had had a mother that would tuck them in at night. They'd been lost, and he'd given them a place to live. Pearl—she meant a lot to all of the boys. But they weren't around her enough.

He'd thought a lot about that over the last couple of days. What would *he* have been like if his mother had stuck around? Would he still have had such bad luck with women? Or would everything have been different?

What if he was wrong, keeping girls off the ranch?

What if Taylor was right, and he was teaching the boys to distrust women?

He moved in a little closer, trying to hear the story she was telling the boys. For a few minutes, he couldn't place it. Then she talked of Atticus, and he knew.

As a boy, he'd loved that book, but he hadn't thought about it in years. Atticus raised two fine children without the benefit of a wife. But he didn't keep his kids away from women. If Zach remembered correctly, there were all sorts of women interfering in the lives of Jem and Scout.

Zach listened for a long time, standing just outside the circle. She was a good storyteller. And the boys sat perfectly still, hanging on her every word. Taylor should have children of her own; she would be a great mother. Strong, independent, clever. Gentle as the night air. Soft and warm and nurturing. The kind of mother who would never leave her children, no matter what.

He'd better go check on the cattle. Stories were fine for the young ones, but he had responsibilities.

He walked toward the corral where Carlos watched over the horses. Taylor's voice followed him for a long while. When it was gone, he felt the loss deeply.

Chapter Twelve

It was late by the time Taylor followed Zach past the chuck wagon, and past the corral of horses. There, sitting in a private little corner, was the tent she'd be sleeping in. Her flashlight also illuminated Zach's sleeping bag lined up in front of the tent opening. "So you're the keeper of the castle, eh?" she said.

He nodded. "Never know when those dragons are going to attack."

"And you don't think I could slay my own dragons?"

"Sure you could. But I'd feel a lot better knowing you won't have to."

"It's too late to argue. Good night, Zach."

He nodded again as she stepped over his bag and went into the tent. It was roomier than she'd thought. She pointed the flashlight down, and she saw that her sleeping bag was open atop several blankets, with two more blankets on top of that. She wasn't sure who'd brought all those blankets, but she didn't need them.

She stuck her head out of the tent, and almost hit Zach in the leg. "Excuse me?"

He knelt down so they were at eye level. "Yes?"

"The blankets. Don't the boys need them?"

"Everyone's squared away."

"But there are so many."

"All for you."

"Okay," she said. "But heavens." She withdrew back into the tent. There was a small lantern next to her pillow, which she fiddled with until it lit. Much easier than using the flashlight. She put it down, and turned to her night kit.

She'd washed—at least her face—outside, using some warmed water provided by Stu. If she'd been with the others, she'd have slept in her clothes, but since she had the tent, it would be much more comfortable to climb into her big sleep shirt.

As she started to undress, her gaze went to the front of the tent. Shadows. She stilled her hands on the bottom of her T-shirt. Zach was right outside. The way she was situated, the light would beam her shadow on the front of the tent. He wouldn't see details, but he'd see her undress.

She went over to turn the lamp off, but then she hesitated. After all, Zach had seen her in her bathing suit. This wasn't going to reveal any more. Less, actually. It was just a shadow, for heaven's sake. She put the lamp down again.

He was probably in bed already, anyway. He wouldn't have undressed—just taken off his boots and his hat, then crawled into the warmth of his bag, where he'd more than likely closed his eyes and conked out in five seconds. So what was she worried about?

She lifted her T-shirt off, and then folded it neatly before she put it in her backpack. Reaching behind, she unclasped her bra. She had it halfway off when she realized what she was doing.

She wanted Zach to see her.

She wanted Zach to *want* her.

There was no use denying it, although she'd never admit it to another living soul. She was undressing in a blatant attempt to make the man *outside* want to come *inside*.

She'd never have done it, except that they were so far from the others. The only reason she knew they weren't in some park was the constant sound of the cattle moving and braying.

Just admitting the truth to herself made her cheeks flush with embarrassment, and she turned so she faced the back of the tent. What kind of fool was she? Sure, she was attracted to him, but she knew better! It was wrong—completely and utterly wrong. But knowing that didn't stop her from wishing.

The truth was, she wanted him.

The thought had started back at the campfire. She'd seen him standing on the outside of the circle when she was telling her story. Standing so tall and so beautiful with the firelight playing on his face. It was a strange sort of feeling, one she'd never had before. Oddly enough, she'd felt as though she were telling a bedtime story to their children, which was absurd, as the youngest of the boys was seventeen. That didn't seem to matter, though. She just kept right on imagining herself as Zach's woman. Imagining him taking her to bed after the others were asleep.

And now that they were alone—away from the boys, from Charlie and Stu—she was trying to seduce the one man she knew was wrong for her.

Although, even that wasn't so clear anymore. There were lots of things about Zach that surprised her. His consideration for the boys. His kindness. His gentleness. Before she'd come to his ranch, she'd been positive that no cowboy in the world could have those qualities. Now she had to rethink her position.

It didn't matter, though. Soon enough she'd be back in the city, in the civilized world, where people worked in offices, and went home at five, and didn't have to get up before dawn. Where a person didn't have to use a creek to bathe.

Which reminded her—she'd better get some work done on her article. It had changed tone so much that she'd had to restart the darn thing three times. It was no longer the utter condemnation that she'd planned. It wasn't all praise, either. Actually, she was happier with it now. It was more balanced. She'd even mentioned some of the things that were wonderful about being a cowgirl. Now that she wasn't so sore, the riding was great. The sense of common purpose, and the willingness to work hard, were both things she hadn't considered before. Probably because she'd never fit in before.

She got her sleep shirt out of her bag and pulled it on. Only then did she slip her jeans off. If Zach was looking, he wasn't going to see much—which was all for the best. If he did come to her, she knew she wouldn't turn him away. But he wouldn't come to her.

She got her brush out and started on her hair, which she'd worn up under her hat. It felt good, and she kept on brushing while she looked for her notebook and her pen. She wouldn't stay up late. Dawn came too quickly, and she needed her rest. But writing a few pages, now, while the beginning of the drive was so fresh in her mind, was a good idea.

She put her brush away, and went to her sleeping bag. It wasn't cold enough for her to get in yet. Instead, she sat cross-legged, and adjusted the lamp so she could see to work.

The words came easily. The sounds of the herd were an excellent accompaniment, and she found herself writing more about the people than about the activities. A page about the boys—each just becoming clear and distinct to her—and then she started writing about Zach.

She began with cool detachment, just going over his job responsibilities and his relationship with the boys, but somewhere on page two, it shifted into far more personal territory.

Personal and intimate.

He was more like the cowboys she'd dreamed about

as a teenager than the cowboys she'd actually known. But this infatuation for him really had her attention. It was just infatuation, of that she was sure, because she knew better than to fall in love with a guy like Zach. He was still a cowboy, and she was still determined to be a city girl. The twain weren't about to meet.

But wouldn't it be nice if they could get together on a temporary basis? One night, for example? *This* night?

She shifted on her sleeping bag, far too aware of how her body had responded to the words on the page. Although it had nothing to do with the article, she wrote about the hot tub, about the kiss in the kitchen. No detail was too small. She wanted to remember everything. To savor it for a long time to come. But mostly, she wished that he wasn't outside her tent, but here, with her, and that he wanted the same thing she did.

She heard something at the entrance to the tent, and she looked up. Writing about Zach had conjured him somehow, because there he was, his head and shoulders poking inside.

"I'm sorry," he said. "I knocked. You didn't answer."

"Knocked?"

"I did the best I could."

"It's all right. What's up?"

"You. It's late. We have to get up awfully early."

"What time is it?"

"Close to midnight. Everyone's asleep."

"You aren't."

He nodded. "I know. I can't."

"Insomnia?"

"Too many distractions," he said. Then he looked at her for a long while, as if making a decision. Finally, he said, "Can I come in?"

She hesitated, but not for long. It was only a coincidence that he'd come to her tent just as she'd been writing about him. But even so, her heart beat faster than it should have. "Sure," she said, putting her notebook and pen back in her bag.

He came in, but he was too tall to stand upright. He chose a spot next to her sleeping bag and sat down. She noticed his gaze on her legs, and then she realized what a show she was giving him. Her sleep shirt was all the way up on her thighs, and from where he was sitting, he could probably even see her panties.

She pulled the material over her legs.

"Thanks," he said.

"Pardon?"

"Nothing," he said, not looking at her, but instead staring at her open backpack. "You have everything you need?"

"Yes, I'm fine."

"Tomorrow morning, after breakfast, I'd like you to herd the horses with Carlos."

"Okay, that's fine."

"The boys—they all like you a lot."

"Zach?"

He looked up at her.

"What's this about?"

"Nothing. I was just… Nothing. Go on to sleep. We have a lot to do tomorrow." He started to get up, but she put her hand on his arm to stop him. He froze.

"Sit down," she said, not releasing her hold. "And tell me why you came in here."

He obeyed—the first part at least. He sat down, closer this time. His leg touched hers, and the heat coming from him made her conscious of how cold the night had become.

"I shouldn't have bothered you," he said, his voice so soft that she had to strain to hear him.

"You're not. I'm not bothered at all."

"You should be," he said, looking from her hand to her eyes. "You should be kicking me the hell out."

"Why is that?"

"Don't make me tell you."

"But I want to hear it."

He narrowed his eyes. "You're a cruel woman, Taylor."

"Now, what have I ever done to you to make you say such a thing?"

His hand covered hers, but it didn't linger there. He moved it to her leg. The moment he touched her, she became incredibly aware of how little she was wearing. Yes, it was more than her bathing suit, but this was different. She was in her "bedroom," such as it was, and in her nightgown, brief as it was. The material of her sleep shirt didn't hide much. She knew without looking that he could see she was aroused.

Breathing as hard as she was didn't help, either. But she couldn't calm down. Her senses were on full alert; every nuance mattered.

It was the kitchen, ten times over, because this time she knew she wasn't going to stop him.

"You knew about the shadows," he said. "You knew it, and you knew I was watching."

"What's cruel about that?"

"I was out there. You were in here."

"But that's not true anymore, is it?"

"Don't joke about this, Taylor."

She took his hand from her leg and brought it up to her lips. She kissed his palm, then she brought that rough, callused, beautiful hand to her breast. The second he touched her, she gasped, unprepared for the wave of physical pleasure that swept through her.

Zach moaned, the sound low and guttural. He moved, very quickly, and she found herself in his arms, leaning back, looking up into his face. Staring at the desire in his eyes. Wanting him more than reason allowed.

He kissed her slowly.

She let herself relax in his arms, savoring the clean taste of him and the wicked things his tongue was doing. She kissed him back, making him moan once more, and then he pulled away.

"What's wrong?" she asked, surprised, barely able to get the words out.

"Are you sure this is what you want?" he asked.

"I wouldn't have asked you in here if it wasn't," she said.

He went to touch her arm, but he didn't make contact. "I want you more than I've wanted any woman in my life," he said. "But I don't want to lie to you. I don't want to hurt you."

"I know this isn't about love," she said, running her fingers through his hair, loving the feel of him more than she could ever have guessed. "This is for tonight. One night. I don't expect more."

He looked at her through worried eyes. "It's okay to say no. I'll respect you either way."

She laughed. "Leave it to a cowboy to worry about my reputation. Relax, Zach. I'm not in the habit of doing this, but I'm also a grown woman, fully capable of making a decision of this magnitude."

"Don't make fun."

"I'm not," she said. "And I thank you for being concerned. But now, what I want you to do is shut up and kiss me."

He smiled a little. "I'm awfully glad you said that, 'cause it was gonna be harder than hell to leave."

"So stay," she said. Then she pulled his head down to continue the kiss.

He complied in a way that swept her doubt aside. She'd told him the truth. Just not all of it. The only thing that worried her about making love to Zach was that once she'd crossed the line, she wouldn't be able to retreat. It could only be this one time. As soon as they got back to the ranch, she was leaving, and the only time she'd ever see Zach again would be at Frankie's wedding. There would be no courtship. No flowers. No rings. No future.

But if she trusted herself, and trusted Zach, there would be one very incredible, very sweet memory. Which was more than she could say about the only other man she'd been with.

There was something honest and good about being with Zach, facing up to her desire. Taking pleasure in knowing how much he wanted her.

As long as she kept things in perspective, this was going to be something she'd treasure forever.

His hands moved down to her breast, and all cogent thought slipped away. Sighing deeply, she started her own exploration of the stunning male body she'd dreamed of since she'd given him that massage. She'd rubbed his back and his shoulders, and now it was time to pay homage to his chest. At least for now. But soon, his chest wouldn't be enough, and she'd have to find out what the cowboy was like underneath his Levis.

ZACH COULDN'T believe that she was in his arms. He'd fought the desire to come into her tent harder than he'd fought the wildest stallion, but it hadn't worked. She'd tormented him by undressing that way, her silhouette so clear that he felt he was inside the room with her. But a shadow wasn't enough. He needed to feel her skin, to taste her lips. He needed to be inside her.

Now, he had to slow it down. He didn't want to

rush and ruin things. This was going to be his only time with her, and he wanted everything to be perfect.

It helped that she smelled so sweet. That her mouth was so warm and willing. That her breast fit in his palm as if it were made for him. And he still wanted more.

Reaching down to the hem of her sleep shirt, he lifted the material up, watching as her thighs were revealed, then her little white bikini panties. He had to stop, to relearn how to breathe.

Then she did the most incredible thing. She moved his hand so it cupped the junction of her thighs. He felt the heat of her, and, as she moved her hips, he felt the need in her.

There was no choice anymore. He had to be in this woman. He had to taste her everywhere. He gently moved her aside, and started undressing.

The whole time, Taylor watched. Looking at his body with the same hunger he felt in her eyes. He wanted her to like what she saw—to forgive the scars and the wounds that marked him as the cowboy he was. He knew she didn't like what he did. But right now, he wasn't a cowboy. He was a man. A man with a need so real that the end of the world couldn't stop him.

Chapter Thirteen

Taylor watched as Zach took off his shirt, mesmerized not only by his physical presence but by the knowledge of what they were about to do. It was so incredible. She was going to make love with a man she'd only known a week. A man she'd disliked so much when she'd met him that the thought of being like this with him was unthinkable. He'd changed her mind. Not because he'd tried to make her like him. She knew for a fact that hadn't been on his agenda at all. He'd changed her mind by his actions, just by being who he was.

As he reached for his belt, she thought about Frankie and Lori. Oh, what they'd say if they knew what she was about to do. She'd never live it down.

But for the first time ever, she could understand why they'd chosen the men they had. Cal was a good man, made that way with the help of Zach. The fact that he was a cowboy didn't make him a louse. It still wasn't going to be easy for Frankie, but if she loved him, they could make it work.

Thoughts of Frankie vanished as Zach unbuttoned his jeans. He got to his knees, and then he crouched, so he could take off his pants.

She couldn't stay still anymore. While he finished undressing, she lifted her sleep shirt off, baring her breasts to his view. His sharp intake of breath told her he liked what he saw.

She stood, and in one swift motion, she was completely naked in front of him. And he was naked, too.

The light from the small lamp created shadows and hid some things from view, but she saw enough. He was beautiful. Rough, worn, strong. His was a body that had been worked long and hard, and had paid the price of the kind of physical labor he did every day. Which made it all the more masculine and exquisite.

He bent down and opened the sleeping bag. She knelt again, and then she lay down, holding her hand out to pull him down with her.

First, though, he turned the lamp very low, creating an intimacy in which they could see each other, but only just. Then he joined her, pulling the blankets on top of them. She wished it hadn't gotten so cold. She would have preferred no covers at all.

It didn't matter, though, when he kissed her. When he put his arm around her back and pulled her close. Feeling him was enough. Feeling the muscles and the flesh, and the hard evidence that he wanted her as much as she wanted him.

She reached down and grasped him, wanting to know this part of him with her hands first. His eyes closed, but it didn't stop his hands from roaming over her body. He touched her the way a blind man would, his fingers exploring every detail. Then he captured her mouth in a kiss.

She kissed him back, so thrilled with the taste of him and the feel of him that she could barely contain herself. She wanted to hurry, but she never wanted this to end. His hand had moved down to her center, and he moaned as he touched her with a feather-light caress. Then he slipped his fingers inside her. Without a conscious thought she moved her hips, so he went deeper.

"I can't believe how good you feel," he whispered. "How hot and wet."

"Zach, please," she said, not sure what she was begging for.

He groaned as he helped her onto her back. She lost him for a moment, but he returned quickly, ripping open a condom packet. Another brief wait while he put it on, and then he was truly with her again. He moved between her legs, the muscles in his arms bulging, holding him up above her so she could look him in the eyes.

He kept her steady with his gaze as he slipped inside her. She gasped at his entry, electrified by the sensations that ran from her core to every nerve ending in her body. He didn't ease up. Instead, he pushed in, filling her, until he was in her completely. It had been a long time for her, yet she couldn't remember ever feeling quite this way before.

He grew still. She tried to do the same, but she wasn't as strong as he was. She had to move. Her hips had to encourage him, her hands had to touch him. She was helpless.

"If you keep moving like that, it's all going to be over too soon."

"No," she said. "I don't want it to ever end."

"Then stop moving."

"I can't."

"Oh," he groaned. He closed his eyes and then his hips started to move. Slowly at first, then faster. Taylor wrapped her legs around him, feeling his penetration deepen.

He looked at her once more, then he bent his head to take a kiss as his tempo evened out into a steady, maddeningly perfect rhythm. Kissing him back sent her over the edge. She cried out even as she kissed him, and pushed her hips up until she couldn't go any farther. Then she felt him tremble. His low moan started as he increased his pace, then, holding himself rigidly still, he came.

The moment was unlike anything she'd experienced before. Not just physically—although that was unbelievable—but emotionally. She'd shared something profound with Zach, something she hadn't expected to. As he let himself down, careful not to crush her, she realized what it was. She'd let him in. Trusted him completely. That was the difference, of course. She'd never fully trusted Ben. He'd been kind to her, and he'd been a good lover, but she'd always held a little bit of herself back. She'd never come with him, at least not without a lot of help. But with Zach, she had given all of herself, trusting that he wouldn't hurt her, or use her vulnerability against her.

Why? Why was this man so different?

"You okay?"

She turned to look at him. His face had relaxed, but he still had a thin sheen of sweat on his forehead. His hand was on her stomach, and his leg crossed over hers. She felt as though she were in a wonderful cocoon. His arms, his whole body—they were there to shield her from the world. She liked it entirely too much. "I'm just grand," she said.

"Grand?"

"Grand, satisfied, content, tired. I don't think there's one word that's accurate enough."

"You're a writer. You're supposed to know the right words."

"Okay. I feel *gratisfied*. How's that?"

His lips quirked. "I like it."

"I'll call Webster first thing when we get back."

"Good. And be sure and give me half the credit."

"Why? I came up with the word."

"But I made you feel that way."

"Okay, you win. Shared credit."

He tossed the tousled blankets over them, covering them from the chest down. "You're chilly," he said.

"I'm okay. I was pretty warm there for a while."

"Yeah, me too." He laid his head down on her shoulder, and she idly petted his hair.

"Isn't this crazy?" she said. "I mean, who would have thought?"

"Not me."

"I mean, I didn't like you very much when I first met you."

"I don't believe you."

"What?"

"I don't believe you. Everybody likes me. I'm a great guy."

"And modest, too."

"Yep."

She yanked a strand of hair, and he yelped, "Hey!"

"You deserved that. Such arrogance!"

"You're the one who showed up with the giant chip on your shoulder. It's only because I'm a sucker for a pretty face that I let you stay at the ranch at all."

"Oh, you're so full of yourself. I was invited by Pearl, remember?"

"But it's *my* playground."

"So we've determined."

He was quiet for a while, but his hand kept rubbing her tummy, which turned out to be just about the best feeling in the world.

"We should go to sleep," she said, wanting him to talk her out of it. "Tomorrow's going to be here soon."

"Yeah. It's gonna be a rough one. A lot of territory to cover." His hand stilled, but she took it and made him rub again.

"Right," she said, settling against him more comfortably. "We're gonna be tired."

"Exhausted."

"On the other hand, maybe this is just what we needed. You know. To get rid of all that tension."

"Tension?"

"Sure," she said. "I've noticed you've been a little snippy. It's understandable. This is a big deal, this drive."

"Snippy?"

"You've got all the boys to worry about, and the cattle. And then there's the whole thing with your back."

"Snippy?"

"So this was probably just what the doctor ordered. You're so relaxed, you'll probably sleep like a baby."

"*Snippy?*"

"You know what I meant."

"I've never been snippy a day in my life."

She sighed. "Sorry. Forgive me. You weren't snippy. You were ornery as a varmint what's been caught in a bear trap."

"Oh, you're asking for it now."

"Really?" She smiled at him. "Cool."

Zach shook his head. "What am I supposed to do with you?"

She shrugged. "Seems like you're doing just fine."

His face grew serious and he stared at her as if seeing her for the first time. "Are we crazy?"

Taylor nodded. "I think that's a given."

"I'm not kidding, Taylor. I know we said this was a one-time event…but dammit, maybe we were being a little hasty."

"Oh, no. Do not go there. I feel far too wonderful to add guilt to the mix."

His hand slid down from her tummy until he definitely got her full attention. She closed her eyes, reveling in the intimate touch.

"We should sleep," she whispered.

"In a minute."

"We're going to be sorry tomorrow."

"It's already tomorrow."

"Oh, yeah. Ooh, right there."

"Like that?"

She nodded, not wanting to talk anymore. She reached over and brushed the back of her hand across his cheek. Then she kissed him, very softly, on the lips. "If you don't stop right now, I'm not going to let you stop."

"Right. We should go to sleep."

"My point exactly."

Then he kissed her, and sleep didn't come for a long, long time.

HE WOKE BEFORE the sun came up. It was cold outside her tent, and his first thought was regret that he hadn't just stayed there next to her. His second thought was regret that he'd gone into her tent at all.

He'd left just after two, so exhausted that he could barely see straight. But he hadn't gone to sleep. Instead, he'd heated some water and brought half of it back to Taylor's tent so she could wash up. He'd used the other half.

Then he'd fallen asleep so quickly, he didn't remember his head touching the ground. He hated to wake Taylor, but there wasn't much choice. He got up and stretched, then decided to let her sleep a little longer. He'd go put on the coffee, if Stu hadn't beaten him to it.

After rolling up his sleeping bag, he went to the chuck wagon. Sure enough, Stu was there, and the coffee was on the fire. There were also several pots of water, some of which would be used for washing, some for oatmeal.

"Morning, boss," Stu said. "Five more minutes on the coffee."

"I'll go get Taylor," Zach said.

"No rush. I've got breakfast handled. Although I could use some help cleaning up."

"She'll be here." Zach didn't want to show her any favoritism. The boys already had it in their minds that he and Taylor were more than friends, if the impromptu singing of "Feelings" yesterday was any indication. He didn't want to encourage the idea. As it was, her presence had undermined some of his stricter rules, and he was determined to underplay her role here as much as possible. No need to get the boys all excited. They had a lot of work to do, and they didn't need to be any more distracted than they already were.

Now, if only he could stop thinking about her, everything would be just fine. But he had the feeling that that was easier said than done.

He'd been a fool last night. One big giant fool. He should never have gone in that tent. Why he'd thought being with her once would get her out of his system, he didn't know. In the light of day, the flaw in his theory was certainly easy to see. But last night, he hadn't been thinking with his brain.

He'd been so certain that he was immune to her. That he could make love to her without feeling anything more than relief. To say he was wrong was an understatement.

Somehow, over the last few days, Taylor Reed had gotten under his skin. He'd had no more control of himself last night than the youngest of his boys. His hormones had driven him to her bed, but now he could see that it was far more than active hormones he was dealing with. For the first time ever, he'd actually considered taking a wife.

Which was just plain nuts. Not only was he crystal clear on how Taylor felt about cowboys and ranches, but a wife was the last thing he needed. For the past few years he'd made damn sure that he avoided any temptations. It was dangerous to think that his luck had changed, that he could bring a woman into his life and not have to pay the consequences. Despite Pearl's belief that things had changed, he had no intention of testing the theory out. From his mother on down, only one woman hadn't brought some kind of disaster along with her. That woman was Pearl. The log falling on his back wasn't just an accident. It was part of the curse that came along with any female. He was just lucky it hadn't killed him.

More important, he was lucky none of the boys had been hurt. Not yet, at least. But they had four more days to go.

He took a pot of warm water and headed back to Taylor's tent. At least he'd gotten some perspective again. Last night was last night. It was great, sure, but it didn't mean anything. Taylor was just passing through. It didn't matter that he'd grown to like her. He liked liquor, but it wasn't good for him, so he avoided it.

He got to her tent. "Taylor?"

He didn't hear anything. He bent down until he could stick his head into the tent opening. She was sound asleep on her side. The thing was, the blankets had moved down, revealing her arm, her shoulder, her breasts.

His groin tightened immediately. He wanted her just as badly as he had last night. His private little pep talk hadn't made one bit of difference. She was the most beautiful thing he'd ever seen. Just looking at her was enough to chase all his good sense away.

"Morning."

He hadn't seen her open her eyes. No wonder, with her being half naked. "I brought you some water."

"Thanks." She sat up, not bothering to cover herself. She just stretched and yawned, and he couldn't keep his gaze on her face. He also couldn't keep his body from responding. The pressure on his jeans grew tight, and it was all he could do not to toss the pot of water outside and say "the hell with the drive."

"Were you waiting for a tip?" she asked.

"Huh?"

"The water. Do I have to pay for it?"

He realized that she'd reached for the pot, but he hadn't moved. Embarrassed, he handed it over, making sure to avoid looking at the danger zone.

"Thanks."

"Yeah," he said. "Coffee's almost ready," he murmured. Then he got out of there. He heard her laugh, and cursed himself for being the biggest idiot in Wyoming.

TAYLOR SHIVERED in the morning air, and quickly began to wash. It was thoughtful of Zach to have awakened her this way, but it was nothing compared to his consideration last night. It had been so late, and yet he'd taken the time to heat up the water and bring it to her, when all he'd wanted to do was get to sleep.

Yet another mark in his favor. This was getting ridiculous. How was she supposed to write a scathing article when the subject was turning out to be a teddy bear? Worse than that, how was she supposed to leave when he made her feel like this? Wanton and sexy and pretty? She'd seen his reaction to her, and she had to admit that she liked it. Memories of last night made her shiver even more than the morning air, as she dried off and started to dress.

He'd surprised her in many ways, but again it was his consideration that really threw her for a loop. The one thing she'd been certain of, and the one thing that had made her so sure that Frankie was making a mistake, was that cowboys only thought of themselves. Zach had made her question that. Not just because he was a thoughtful lover, or because he brought her hot water. It went deeper than that. The truth was, he put the safety and the training of the boys first. He didn't just *talk* about making a difference, he *did* something about it.

The real surprise was that making love with him had made her realize that he was a man of honor. That she could trust him. She'd imagined a lot of consequences, but not this one.

She stood up and put on a fresh pair of jeans, then got down to the task of putting everything away. She rolled up her sleeping bag and folded the blankets. Finally, she put everything outside and started to take down the tent.

Cal came over to help. Then Jesse joined them. The job was done in half the time, and the boys took everything to the chuck wagon. When she got there, she saw that everyone else was already eating breakfast. She went over to Stu and apologized for being so late. He smiled, handed her a cup of coffee, and told her to go eat.

At the campfire, the boys had left her a space right next to Zach. She sat down, afraid to look at him, afraid that she'd do something that would spill the beans about last night. He didn't look at her, either.

How in the world was she going to get through the next four days, when she couldn't even sit near him without blushing like a schoolgirl? One thing was certain. She'd been stupid to think she could make love to him and then just walk away. Not when he made her feel like this. She cursed herself for being the biggest idiot in Wyoming.

Chapter Fourteen

Zach was tired. Bone tired. It had been a hard three days, but finally the cattle had all been immunized and were now safely ensconced in the high pasture. The boys had done well. To a man, they'd done their share, and they'd done it right. His fears about having Taylor along had been unfounded. No one had gotten hurt. Matter of fact, Taylor had turned out to be a big help. She'd done far more than cook or take night watch. She'd roped, inoculated, and generally been a skilled cowhand.

They'd be heading home tomorrow. Tonight would be something special. He'd planned it before they even left. Stu had some treats in store, and he'd made up some blue ribbons for the boys, just like the ones they gave out at the rodeo. It would be an early night, that much was for sure. Every one of the gang was exhausted. They'd go to sleep just after sunset, and be on the road back by first daylight. By tomorrow night, they'd be home, sleeping in their own beds. And it would be his last night with Taylor.

He found it hard to believe that he was upset about that fact, but he was. Something had happened over the course of ten days. The last thing he ever would have expected. He'd come to depend on a woman. Depend on her for a hundred things, but mostly just to be there. To make him smile, to make him angry. To make him feel relaxed and easy.

Not to mention the incredible nights spent in her tent.

She was a lover unlike any he'd ever known. And dammit, he didn't want her to leave.

The problem was, nothing had changed. Not as far as Taylor was concerned. She still had another life, and a future he couldn't be a part of. The fact that they had hit it off so well didn't alter her dislike of ranching, or make her want to give up her dreams. Despite the fact that she seemed to be enjoying herself, she hadn't told him otherwise. That was the thing that struck him in the gut. She hadn't changed her mind. So asking her to stay would be asking too much. The life he had to offer was hard, with no rewards other than getting the job done. She deserved so much more.

He just couldn't get over how happy she seemed. She was born for this work. But maybe he just *wanted* to see that.

Then again, she was always laughing and joking with the boys. She sure as hell looked like she belonged. Not a touch of makeup on her face, yet she was achingly beautiful. The worst part of it was that he kept imagining her working with him on the ranch.

Being a part of the roundup, of the livestock shows. Waking up next to her in bed. Having his children. He still wasn't about to let girls on the ranch, but Taylor wasn't a girl. She was a woman.

"You gonna sit there spinning wool for the rest of the afternoon?"

He looked up to see Taylor right next to him. She was petting Paladin's neck. That mean old horse had turned into a pussycat in Taylor's hands. Zach knew just how he felt. "What's up?"

"We've got a few hours till dinner, and I thought we could work with the boys on some rodeo techniques. What do you say?"

"Aren't they all too tired?"

"They're kids, Zach. It's only us old fogies who are beat."

"I don't know."

"Come on. Don't be a stick-in-the-mud. You help Johnny with his roping, and I'll help Jesse with his barrel racing. I think some of the other boys want to practice, too."

"What about Stu? Doesn't he need help?"

"I've got cleanup duty tonight."

He thought about it for another moment, but he couldn't think of one good reason why they shouldn't do it. "All right."

She broke out in a smile that made his chest tighten. "Thanks, boss," she said. Then she rode off toward the pack of boys on the other side of the corral.

He urged Falcon to follow. He didn't much feel like

roping, but he couldn't tell her that. Not when she wanted it so much. The truth was, if she'd asked him to rope the moon, he'd have done it for her.

He reached the boys and saw that Pete and Cal were out putting bedrolls and spare saddles in a cloverleaf pattern across a level piece of pasture land. They'd double as barrels. Several feet to the right, three of the other boys were putting together a makeshift enclosure so they could bring a calf in.

He headed toward the enclosure where Johnny waited. Little Danny, Eddie and Eric were also there, all of them holding their ropes, ready to go.

Zach waited while they pulled a calf from the herd and brought her to the pen. Then he told Johnny to go on ahead. It took the boy seven tries, and a lot of frustration, but he finally roped the calf, pretty as you please. The rest of the boys shouted encouragement, and when the deed was done they all whooped like Johnny had won at the Olympics.

All the while, Jesse had been riding his horse around the makeshift barrels. He hadn't had a clean ride yet, and when Zach looked over this time, he saw Taylor take Paladin through his paces. Damn if she didn't ride him like he'd been born for the task. Charlie was watching, and he caught Zach's eye. Zach shook his head; Charlie grinned. They'd both been so sure that Taylor couldn't handle a horse like Paladin. She'd proved them wrong.

Her run was clean. The boys clapped and hollered. Taylor looked beautifully triumphant.

All Zach could think about was the fact that this was so temporary. She was leaving. Several of the boys were getting ready to take off for college. Sure, he'd still have Charlie and Stu and Carlos, but the rest of them were only here for a little while. Then they'd go off to other ranches, other jobs.

His gaze went back to Taylor, and he thought about what it would be like if Jesse were their son, instead of a boy just passing through. Zach realized he wanted a son. Someone who would carry on at the ranch after he was gone. Someone who would love the land the way he did. He also realized that he wanted to have that son with Taylor.

He cursed, and Little Danny looked at him funny. Zach ignored the boy, and forced himself to watch Eric as the boy fought it out with the wily calf. But the image of Taylor carrying his child wouldn't leave him be.

ZACH MET STU behind the chuck wagon. The cook handed him a plate covered with tinfoil, and Zach nodded his thanks. He slipped away, anxious to get to Taylor's tent. She'd like his little surprise, he thought. Fudge brownies, made especially for her. He made his way easily, as the moon was full and so brilliant that it made the whole world shimmer with pale blue light. He wished they didn't have to stay in her tent. Tonight, he would have liked to take her under the stars. Under that huge moon.

Just as he was passing the corral, Charlie shouted

his name. Zach turned. Charlie was waving him over, and he looked worried. Zach glanced at the tent once, then headed toward his foreman.

"We got a problem," Charlie said, even before Zach reached his side.

"What's up?" Zach asked, his gut tightening.

"It's Jesse. He's hurt."

"How bad?"

"Come on," Charlie said. "I've got him just outside the traps. I don't want to wake the others."

Zach hurried after him, and as they passed the chuck wagon, he put the brownies down on the running board, then got the first-aid kit out. Then he and Charlie headed for the cow pen. "What happened?"

"The damn fool kid fell off the gate, and he got stepped on."

"What was he doing on the gate?"

"You'll have to ask him that."

"How bad is he?"

"I don't know. Cal's with him." Charlie broke into a run, and Zach did too, his heart thumping like a kettle drum in his chest. By the time they reached Cal and Jesse, Zach had imagined the worst. Cal had his flashlight on Jesse's hand. It was badly swollen and red, and his little finger was bleeding.

Zach crouched down next to the boy. "Is that the only place you're hurt?"

"Yeah," Jesse said. "I'm sorry." His voice was strong and even, which made Zach feel a little better.

He lifted Jessie's hand, and the boy winced. "Can you move your fingers?"

Jesse curled his fingers into a loose fist, then opened them again. From what Zach could see, nothing was broken. The boy was swollen pretty badly, but it didn't look worse than that. "Let's get back to camp," he said. "I'll bandage you there, after we clean you up."

Cal and Zach helped Jesse up. The boy held his hand as steady as he could while they walked. "What happened?" Zach asked.

"I fell."

"I know that. Why were you on the gate?"

"I was practicing my roping."

"On the herd? At night?"

"Yeah."

"Why?"

"I didn't want anyone to know. It was supposed to be a surprise."

"Some surprise."

"I know, Zach. I'm sorry."

"Sorry doesn't cut it, buddy," he said. "You could have started a stampede, you know that? Dammit, you could have gotten yourself killed."

"I—"

"Forget it," Zach said. "It doesn't matter now. We just need to get you fixed up."

They reached the campfire, and Charlie went to get some hot water to wash Jesse's hand. Zach had Jesse sit down near the light from the fire. He opened the first-aid kit, and got out the antiseptic, a gauze bandage, some aspirin.

As Charlie came back, Zach looked toward Taylor's tent. She would be waiting. Expecting him. But he couldn't go yet. She'd understand once she knew what had happened.

He got to work on Jesse's hand, grateful that the damage wasn't worse. He didn't bother to ask Jesse who he was trying to impress with his roping. The answer was clear. Dammit, they were so close. One more day. He'd almost believed that the curse had been lifted, that the bad luck wouldn't plague his ranch anymore.

By the time he was finished and everyone had gone to bed, it was past midnight. Zach headed for Taylor's tent, glad to see the light was still on. When he opened the flap, he saw that Taylor was sound asleep. He debated waking her. But she was so tired, and frankly, so was he. He wished their last night on the drive could have been different, but it was no use crying over spilt milk. He slipped inside the tent and turned off the lantern. Before he left, he fixed her covers. His fingers touched her soft cool skin, and the urge to wake her was strong. He let it go.

ALL DURING the ride back to the ranch, the boys kept asking her what was wrong. They didn't believe her excuse that she was just tired, but after a while they let her be.

She'd learned about Jesse first thing that morning.

Zach apologized, and she'd assured him that she understood. But she didn't. Not that she wanted him to ignore Jesse, but she knew that Charlie and Cal had been with the boy, and that Charlie knew first aid. She knew it was petty and selfish of her to be angry. She tried to talk herself out of it, but she couldn't. She'd wanted so much for their last night to be special. She'd waited and waited, all the while trying to fight off the feeling that she'd been there before. She recognized the disappointment as an old friend. One she'd thought she'd said goodbye to forever.

It wasn't fair, she knew that. Zach had done the right thing. He really had. And yet, the hurt inside her wouldn't go away.

She'd been living in a dream world, that's all. A perfectly ideal situation in which she and Zach were together all day, and especially all night. It wouldn't always be like that. Matter of fact, it would hardly ever be like that. The ranch would come first. Always.

But even while she was saddened by the reality, she had to admit that she understood. Zach was a responsible man. He wouldn't leave her to go out with his buddies to get drunk. He wouldn't leave her to ride the rodeo circuit. But he'd leave her. The reasons would all be valid. There would be no choice.

None of which held a candle to her real dilemma—the one thing her logic couldn't change, that she couldn't rationalize away. She loved him. She loved him so much, it made her realize she hadn't ever loved Ben. And worse, she didn't want to leave. She wanted

Zach to love her back, even though she knew that if he did, it would mess up both their lives.

The whole ride back, the debate inside her raged. Knowing what she knew—that Zach's first priority would always be the ranch—did she want to stay? And if she did, could she risk confessing her feelings to Zach? Admit that she'd been happier on his ranch than she'd been the whole time she'd lived in Houston?

Even if it did turn out that he had feelings for her, what then? Was she really prepared to give up all she'd worked for? Go back to the ranch life—the one thing she'd sworn she'd never do?

And would he bend his rules to let her stay? There was one thing she could never change, and that was the fact that she was a woman.

The frustration was nearly impossible to bear. She did make one decision. She would talk to Pearl when they got back, tell her everything, and ask for her advice about Zach. If Pearl told her that she was barking up the wrong tree, she'd leave quietly. But if Pearl told her to take the risk, she'd do it. She'd shake all the way, but there was too much at stake to let her fears stop her now.

IT WAS SUNSET when they reached the ranch. It took all her strength to take care of Paladin before she went up to the house, but the horse had been so good that she couldn't leave without giving him a good brushing and making sure he was comfortably back in his stall. She knew Zach was doing the same with Falcon. She

thought about talking with him, but she didn't trust
herself yet. Even meaningless conversation seemed too
difficult to pull off while her thoughts were in such
turmoil.

Finally, she headed up to the house to put her things
away. She was desperate for a shower. Then she'd find
Pearl. But she didn't have to go in search of Zach's
aunt; she was standing at the door.

"Welcome home!" she said.

Taylor smiled, genuinely glad to see her. "Howdy,
ma'am," she said in her best cowpoke drawl.

"Is everyone okay?"

"Yep. Well, Jesse hurt his hand, but he's gonna be
just fine. The boys did a wonderful job."

"And Zach?"

"He did a good job, too."

Pearl ushered her in. "That's not what I meant."

"I know. Actually, I have some things to talk to
you about. But I simply must shower. I can't live with
myself even five more minutes this way."

"The towels are ready for you. But before you go,
I have a message for you. It's from your editor."

"Oh?"

"He said to call right away. Whenever you got
back."

Taylor looked at the stairs—the path to a heavenly
shower. But Quentin didn't leave messages like that
lightly. She turned to Pearl. "May I use your phone?
My portable is God knows where."

"Of course."

Taylor walked over to the sideboard and dialed her boss's home phone number. He wouldn't be at work this late.

He launched into the conversation without even one question about her article. But when she heard what he had to say, she understood his excitement.

"Are you serious, Quentin? I get to ride with the presidential press corps? For the whole campaign?"

"Yep. Dan got a job at CNN. He didn't even tell me he was looking, the traitor. So, you're the new junior White House correspondent, kiddo. Congratulations."

"When would I start?"

"As soon as you can get yourself back to town. I've got some friends in Washington who can help you find an apartment."

"Oh, God," she said. "Of course. I'd have to move to D.C."

"What did you think? It's a pretty long commute from Houston to the White House!"

She felt dazed. She'd never dreamed she'd be offered more than congressional hearings. Dan had mentioned that he was looking for another job, but she hadn't known he was this serious about it. It was all so hard to believe.

"Taylor? Have you fainted from joy?"

"No, no. I'm here. Just trying to assimilate all this."

"Well, kiddo, assimilate all you want, but get your ass back here on the double. I'm using stringers, and I want that to stop."

"Thanks, Quentin. Let me call you back in the morning. I'm too tired to think straight."

"Fine. Talk to you then."

She hung up the phone, but she didn't rush upstairs yet. This little bombshell changed everything. Or did it?

Was she prepared to give up the job she'd never dared to hope for...the life she'd dreamed of...to become a cowboy's wife? Of course, she was crazy even thinking that way. Zach had never once indicated that he wanted her to be his wife.

"It sounds like good news," Pearl said.

Taylor turned, having forgotten Pearl was behind her. "It is, I think."

"Oh?"

Taylor told her about the offer. Pearl listened carefully. When Taylor was finished, she touched her arm. "Is this what you want?" she asked.

Taylor didn't answer for a bit. "It's what I've wanted for a long time," she said. She squeezed the older woman's hand. "I need to go get washed up. We'll talk after I get out of the shower, okay?"

Pearl nodded.

"IT SOUNDS LIKE a good job."

Pearl swung around, startled. He hadn't meant to scare her. "Guess you didn't hear me come in," he said.

"No, I didn't. Welcome home. It was a long week without you."

"I missed you, too."

"So you heard?"

He nodded. "Working at the White House. That's a pretty big deal."

"She didn't accept the job."

"She will." He went over and gave his aunt a hug. "I'm gonna go shower, too."

"Good idea," she said, laughing.

"Thanks."

"I only meant that you needed to relax," Pearl said.

"I'll bet." Zach headed toward his room, careful to keep his back straight so that Pearl wouldn't notice anything was wrong. But when he turned the corner, he let his shoulders sag. Damn. A White House job. Who in their right mind would turn that down to live on a ranch? He would, but that's 'cause all he'd ever wanted was right here.

No, that wasn't true anymore. There was something else he wanted. Maybe more than the ranch itself. Maybe more than he'd wanted anything else in his life.

He wanted Taylor.

But he couldn't compete. It was bad enough before. Now, his chances had slid from slim to none.

Chapter Fifteen

Taylor had never enjoyed the pure physical pleasure of a shower more in her life. Although she'd bathed when she was on the trail, it wasn't a satisfying experience. This was bliss.

As she let the hot water work its miracle, she tried to think logically about her next step.

She'd wanted a job in Washington for one heck of a long time. Being the White House correspondent was more than she'd ever hoped for. It was prestigious, it paid well for a journalist, and it was exciting to think of playing with the big boys. Of course, it would take her years to gain respect, to actually become a part of the White House press corps. But she had no doubts that she could do it.

It would mean traveling. A lot. It would be a simple thing to move to Washington. No one in particular would miss her. She had some friends, but not that many. Hell, she didn't even have a cat. Her apartment in Houston, for all her posturing, had been more of a way station than a home. Her job had been a stepping-stone; her friends, acquaintances. Ever since she'd left the ranch at eighteen, she'd been waiting for her real life to begin.

Now, it looked as though it was about to happen. But was this the life she wanted?

She had to face it. In Washington, she'd be married to her job. On the other hand, it was just this side of possible that if she stuck around here, she could be married to Zach.

The nights would be infinitely better with Zach, but what about the days? My God, she'd spent the last few years as the "I Hate Cowboys" poster girl. She'd ridiculed her mother and her sisters for choosing the life she was now contemplating. What did that say about her convictions? About her sanity?

She turned off the hot water and stepped out of the shower, grabbing the soft blue towel from the sink top. Drying herself off quickly, she left the bathroom and got dressed. It was time to talk to Pearl. Although she hadn't known the woman long, she trusted her. And the woman knew Zach better than anyone. If a future with Zach was in the realm of possibility, Pearl would tell her. She'd also tell Taylor if she was wasting her time.

Back in the bathroom, Taylor urged the hair dryer to hurry. She didn't quite finish the job, but it was enough to get by. She didn't bother with makeup. She left the room, and almost ran down the stairs.

When she got to the kitchen, she heard her name—

and Zach's voice. She hesitated, listening. But it was Pearl who spoke next.

"According to Cal and Jesse, Taylor did a wonderful job."

"I'm not denying that," Zach said.

"Then why?"

"I've got my reasons."

"Don't play that game with me, young man."

"It's not a game. All I'm saying is that nothing's changed."

"Nothing?"

"That's right. Girls on the ranch will still be trouble. Jesse got hurt because he was trying to impress Taylor. We were just lucky he wasn't killed."

"Jesse was foolish. It had nothing to do with Taylor."

"It did. The kid is infatuated with her. That made him foolish."

"Are you talking about Jesse? Or yourself?"

"What?"

There was a long pause, and Taylor thought about walking into the kitchen. It wasn't right to stand here and eavesdrop, but it felt wrong to intrude. If she had any manners at all, she'd walk away. But between manners and her future, there was no contest.

"Zach, sit down."

Taylor heard him sigh, then the scrape of two chairs. She moved a little closer to the door frame.

"Honey," Pearl said, "I love you, and I always will. That's why it hurts me to see you isolate yourself like you do. It's not healthy. I admit, you've had some bad luck, but it won't always be that way. Can't you see? She's broken the spell. Let her in, Zach."

"Pearl—"

"No, don't interrupt. You're too smart to let the past ruin your future. I say this with all my love, dear— but get over it. Women are *not* the enemy."

"I know that."

"So why aren't you doing something about it?"

"I thought we were talking about the ranch."

"We were. Now we're talking about you."

"There's nothing to say."

"Nothing?"

"That's right."

"You don't feel anything for her?"

"I like her."

"But?"

"But she's going to Washington. That's all. Look, I've got to go talk to Charlie. I'll be back later."

Taylor dashed past the dining room table and halfway up the stairs before she turned around. Zach came out of the kitchen just as she was again reaching the ground floor. She struggled to look calm, as if she hadn't heard a word. In fact, she even managed a smile.

"Congratulations," he said.

She broadened her smile. "Thanks."

"It sounds like a great career move."

"I hope so."

"Are you still going to finish the article about the ranch?"

She nodded. "Yeah. Although it's changed."

"How do you mean?"

"Let's just say I learned a thing or two while I was here."

"Is that good?"

Her smile faltered, and she just didn't have it in her to fight it. Instead, she started walking, intending to pass him quickly. But then his hand touched her arm. She looked up at him, into his clean-shaven face. His hair was still damp from his shower. His eyes were dark and questioning. Just looking at him broke her heart.

"Is that good?" he asked again.

She nodded. "Yes, Zach. I was wrong about a lot of things."

"Like what?"

"I didn't realize before that being a cowboy could be such a fine thing."

"That *is* a change."

"You're in the right place, Zach. You're doing good things. You're…"

"What?"

She smiled. "You're Gary Cooper. For real."

He looked at her hard. For a moment, she thought he was going to say something, but he just shook his head. He took his hand away and stepped back. "I need to go talk to Charlie," he said.

She watched him go, knowing this was her last

chance. If she didn't say something now, it would be too late. But what was she going to say? *Let me stay? Break all your rules? Trust me, even though I lied about my reasons for being here?*

Let me stay because I love you?

"Zach."

He stopped, but he didn't turn around.

She tried to form the words, but she couldn't. She already knew the answer. It would only humiliate them both to speak it out loud.

"Yes?"

"I just wanted you to know that I had a great time."

"Me, too," he said as he opened the door. "You weren't what I expected."

She laughed. "Funny you should say that."

He turned. "Why?" He took one step in her direction, then stopped. He crossed his arms over his chest.

"You're not what I expected, either. Not at all."

"Well, I suppose that's a compliment."

"It is. Now what about you? Do you still think all women are dangerous?"

He didn't answer her. The smile that had teased his lips turned into a frown. "Yeah, I do."

"Come on, Zach," she said. "Jesse's accident wasn't serious. Nothing life-threatening happened."

"He could have been killed."

"But he wasn't. He's going to be fine. And no one else got hurt."

"I did."

She stopped, closed her eyes. Was he talking about the log falling on his back—or something else?

"It was my own fault," Zach said. "I should have known better."

"Known better about what?" she asked, afraid to hear his answer, praying that he would say that he should have known better than to let her go. Then she looked in his eyes.

"I should have known better than to take you along," he said.

She bit her lip, trying hard to keep from showing what his words were doing to her. It was like being punched hard in the stomach. "I'm sorry, then."

"Don't be," he said fiercely. "Don't *you* be sorry." He took another step, then wavered for a moment. He ran his hand roughly through his hair, then walked up to her—so close that all she had to do was lift her arm and she would touch him.

"I'm not sorry for one thing," he said. "Hurt or no hurt, I'm glad you... And I'm glad we..."

She closed her eyes. "Yes," she whispered. "I'm glad about that, too."

Zach was struggling. She could see it in his brows, in the thin line of his mouth. Finally, he moved, and she felt his lips once more. The kiss was brutal. Angry. His hands gripped her upper arms and squeezed, hurting her. In a few seconds it was over.

"Goodbye, Taylor," he said. Then he walked out the door. She felt the imprint of his fingers for a long time. The imprint of his kiss would last forever.

TAYLOR WROTE at the small desk in her bedroom. She wrote, concentrating as fiercely as she could on the article, willing herself to ignore the fact that Zach was downstairs. That tomorrow, very early, she'd leave this place and never see him again. No, he'd probably be at Frankie's wedding. By that time she hoped the pain would have eased, and she'd be able to look at him without regret.

For now, it was better to stay shut in her room. She'd even had dinner here, telling Pearl that she was too tired to join the others. Pearl had looked doubtful, but she hadn't said anything.

Taylor read over the last paragraph and changed a few words. She glanced at the clock; it was close to midnight. Her eyes burned with fatigue, and the bed behind her beckoned, but she didn't stop.

Finally, at two-fifteen, she finished the article. She read the piece over one last time. It was good. Maybe the best thing she'd ever written. She'd accomplished her goal and told the truth about cowboys. She'd captured a great deal of Zach in the words. His strength. His loyalty. His stubborn streak. She'd also told of his intractability and his old-fashioned beliefs. Mostly, though, she'd captured the spirit of the man who quietly succeeded in something very few people did: he made a difference. He accepted his responsibilities as a member of his community, and he helped change the course of many lives—all for the better. The cowhands might come to Zach as boys, but they left as men.

They learned to work hard, to respect the land, to respect each other.

But she also told of the other cowboys. The kind she'd grown up with. Her bitter memories were just as real as her experience with Zach. She told this tale with a whole new perspective, though. In the end, the truth turned out to be gray. Not black or white. Complex, confusing, and full of contradictions.

She saved her work on the hard drive and on a floppy disk. She carefully labeled the disk, and then she went back to the keyboard. There was one more thing she needed to write before she could go to bed. A letter to Zach. A confession.

There was something else writing the article had made clear to her. It wasn't something she was thrilled about, but it wasn't to be avoided. Not anymore. She'd gone too long blaming others for her unhappiness. Cowboys were just an easy target—something for her to focus all her pain and her hurt on. But she knew now that cowboys were men, just like other men. Some good. Some bad. Some hurtful.

The most difficult realization came when she figured out why she'd been so certain that it was cowboys who'd done her wrong. If it wasn't cowboys who dismissed anyone who wasn't one of their own, then the truth was that her father had dismissed *her*. And Ben had left *her*. Not because they were cowboys, but because they chose not to love her.

If Zach didn't ask her to stay, it wasn't because he

was a cowboy. It was because he didn't love her. That's all.

She'd expected this new awareness to be painful, and it was. But there was more to it than that. For the first time, she was taking responsibility for her choices. Her father did the best he could. She just couldn't be the son he wanted. And Ben? Ben was a nice guy, but not someone she could have been happy with. He was just a way to get her father's attention.

Now, though, there was someone she *could* be happy with. Zach. She felt it in her bones. They would make a great team together. Well, they would have, anyway.

She wrote all of it down, all of it except the last part. Her courage failed her there. But she was glad she'd told so much of the truth. It probably wouldn't matter, but for the record, she wanted Zach to know that knowing him had changed her. Forever.

Finally, she turned off the machine. After she changed into her nightgown, she set the alarm. Then she crawled into bed. But sleep didn't come.

ZACH STOOD on the hill above the house. The spot where he'd first laid eyes on Taylor Reed. It was just after sunrise of what looked to be a beautiful day. But he took no pleasure in the crisp air, or the blue sky. He barely noticed the hawk circling above him.

All he could see was the back end of a taxicab.

All he could remember was the feel of her lips as she'd kissed him goodbye.

All he could feel was a hurt that threatened to swallow him whole.

Even now, he wanted to stop her. To ask her to stay. But he knew what foolishness that would be. She was destined for other things. For a life he could barely imagine. Politics. Power. Prestige. Not getting up at the crack of dawn to see to the horses. Not the long days, the relentless chores. He had so little to offer her. Only his love, and that had never been enough to make anyone stick around.

He turned from the empty road, and walked back to the house. For him, it was just another working day.

TAYLOR STARED out the window, not really seeing. The cab driver had enough sense not to talk to her, and for that she was grateful. She didn't want to make conversation. She was afraid that if she spoke at all, she'd ask him to turn the cab around.

She closed her eyes. Of course, he was there, as clear as if he'd been next to her on the seat instead of miles away on his horse. She remembered every detail of how he'd looked at her coolly as she said goodbye. For a second—no, a fraction of a second—she'd thought she'd seen something more. A wish. A hope. And then again, when she'd kissed him. At first, she'd felt the heat, the electric connection that had been between them from the first day. But then, his lips had grown cold and he'd practically pushed her away.

That, more than anything, forced her into silence now. Zach didn't want her. Oh, she knew he *liked* her.

That sex between them had been extraordinary, and that he respected her. She wasn't blind, she could see all those things. But that didn't mean he loved her. If he did, wouldn't he have asked her to stay?

He hadn't even waited for the taxi to come before he'd left for his chores. At least that had given her time enough to go to his room. To leave a copy of her article. To run her hand over his pillow. To lift his jacket to her face and memorize the scent that was his alone.

At least he hadn't seen her cry. That was something, wasn't it?

HE DIDN'T FIND the computer disk until that night. After dinner, he'd come back to his room to get ready for bed. It was early, but he hadn't slept well the night before. As he unbuttoned his shirt, he noticed it on his desk. It had his name on it, in what he could only surmise was Taylor's handwriting.

He left his shirt open, and went to the office. A few moments later, he'd turned on his computer and slipped the disk in. A few mouse clicks, and he saw what she'd left him. A copy of her article.

He read it three times.

Only then did he read the second file—the one with his name on it.

Dear Zach,
I couldn't leave without telling you what these past two weeks have meant to me. I learned a

great deal. Not just about cattle ranching in Wyoming, but about myself—about my beliefs and my fears. I'd come here expecting to find the kind of cowboys I'd grown up around. What I found instead was you. A totally different breed. A man with a conscience, with a heart. A man with strong ethics and fierce convictions. A good, decent man.

I know now that I had blamed cowboys for a lot of things in my life. The truth isn't so simple. The truth is that cowboys were my scapegoat, a way for me to take the spotlight off my own failings.

I can't do that anymore. I *won't* do that anymore. And while that's painful, I think it gives me a fighting chance for happiness. I owe that to you. You didn't mean to teach me, but you did. I'll never forget that. And I'll never forget you.

For who you are, and who you made me, I thank you.

Taylor.

He read it again, then shut off the computer. He stood up. He wasn't quite so tired anymore. He doubted he could sleep, at any rate. So he buttoned his shirt, grabbed his jacket, and headed out for a walk. He needed to think—long and hard.

Chapter Sixteen

"I'm sorry, Quentin. I just can't come back yet. I need another few days."

Taylor pulled the phone away from her ear as her editor yelled. It didn't matter. She wasn't going to budge on this. If it meant that she lost the job, then so be it. That might even make things easier.

She'd arrived at Lori's half an hour ago, knowing that the decisions she was about to make would affect the rest of her life. She'd been so sure about what she wanted before she'd gone to the ranch. But that had changed. The Washington job was certainly still in the running, but it wasn't the only thing anymore. She needed to think. To talk to her sisters.

Quentin seemed to have run out of curse words, and she brought the phone back to her ear. "Are you done?"

"For the moment."

"I'll call you the day after tomorrow. By then, things here will be straightened out."

"When am I going to get your article?"

"I'll e-mail that to you tonight."

"All right. But dammit, Taylor, do whatever you have to do fast. You're needed here."

She said goodbye, and hung up. It was good to know she was needed somewhere.

"Coffee's ready."

Taylor headed toward the kitchen. Frankie smiled at her, and Taylor could see that she was anxious. She hugged her sister, then took her hand to lead her to the table. Lori was already seated. Three mugs stood in a row next to the coffeepot.

Once the three of them were settled, and the coffee poured, Lori and Frankie turned their attention to Taylor.

"There's something I need to say," Taylor said. "It's about Mom."

Lori looked at Frankie, then back at Taylor. "What?"

"I know why Mom stayed with Dad all those years. Despite the fact that he wasn't home much. I'd always figured she was just happy playing the martyr, but I was wrong. So wrong. She just loved him. That's all. That was enough."

"She did, Taylor," Frankie said. "She loved him, big time."

"I'm just so sorry it took me so long to figure that out. I wish I could have told her."

"It's okay," Lori said, taking her hand. "She knows. I promise."

Taylor swallowed, fighting back tears. "And you

guys will be happy to note that I'm no longer mad at Daddy. I'm sad that we couldn't have been closer, but the anger—it's all gone."

"What happened to you out there?" Frankie asked.

"I'll tell you," Taylor said, "but first, I have this to say about your Cal."

Frankie leaned forward with so much hope in her eyes that Taylor nearly lost it. "I think he's wonderful," she said.

"Really, Taylor? You mean it?"

She nodded. "I give you my blessing. I think you'd be crazy to let him go."

"Oh, my God," Frankie said, laughing. "I knew you'd like him. And he likes you, too. Oh, Taylor, this is just wonderful. He said you were terrific, and that he can't wait till you're his sister-in-law."

Taylor could feel her sister's happiness as if it were her own. It was so clear that Frankie was head-over-heels in love. "I'm glad he realizes that he's found himself a gem."

"What about Zach?"

Taylor turned to Lori. "What?"

"Well? Don't keep us in suspense. What happened with you and Zach?"

Taylor was just about to launch into her story, when she realized what Lori was saying. "You know Zach?"

Lori and Frankie exchanged guilty looks. "I don't exactly know him," Lori said. "But I'd heard about him."

"What's going on here? Why are you blushing, Frankie?"

"Don't blame her," Lori said. "It was my idea."

"But I agreed," Frankie said.

"You'd better tell me what this is about." Taylor leaned back, eyeing her sisters, not liking this one bit.

"It's just that I met Zach when I was working for the hotel. And Cal thinks the world of him."

"And?"

"And we thought you two might hit it off," Lori said.

"So this was a setup? You guys were trying to set me up with a *cowboy?*"

Her sisters nodded in unison. "But we weren't the only ones who had a secret agenda, were we?" Lori teased.

"What's that supposed to mean?"

"Your article."

"How did you…?"

"Quentin called," Frankie said. "Several times. He told Lori all about it."

"He doesn't *know* all about it."

"So you didn't write an exposé on how horrible cowboys are?"

Taylor shook her head. "I didn't. I wrote something completely different."

"What?"

"I'm still not finished with you two, so quit trying to change the subject. Why did you think Zach and I should be together?"

"Because he's all the things you wanted," Lori said simply.

"Pardon me? I must have told you a thousand times that I didn't want anything to do with a cowboy."

"No," Lori said. "You didn't want anything to do with a man like Daddy, or Ben. But I remember all the years when you used to tell me about your perfect man. You described him to a tee—looks, attitudes, interests. When Frankie told me about Zach, it was like hearing about an old friend. At first, I didn't get the connection, but then it came to me. Zach was the man you used to write about. Remember? You wrote all those love stories when you were a kid. You were always the heroine, and the hero was always the same. He was always Zach. We just didn't know it then."

"Why didn't you tell me?"

"You wouldn't have gone, would you?"

She shook her head. "No, you're right. I wouldn't have."

"So are you going to tell us what happened, or not?" Frankie asked.

Taylor sighed. She looked at her hands clasped around her mug. "Your plan didn't work," she said.

"But Pearl said you two... Your tent..."

She looked up sharply at Frankie. "She knew about the tent? She was in on it, too?"

Frankie nodded. "She said everyone was really happy for you. They were all sure you and Zach were going to get married."

"They were wrong," she said.

"You didn't like him?" Lori asked.

Taylor felt her lip quiver, and she willed it to stop. "I liked him. Dammit, I fell in love with him. You were right about that. Only, he didn't fall in love with me."

Taylor wished somebody would say something. If they didn't, she wasn't going to be able to hold back the tears that threatened.

"I'm sorry, honey," Lori said, her voice so full of sympathy that Taylor didn't stand a chance. The first tear fell, and then she couldn't see or speak. All she could do was cry.

She felt Frankie and Lori's arms around her.

"I'm so confused," Frankie said. "Cal was so sure Zach was crazy about you."

"If he was, he would have asked me to stay, wouldn't he?"

Lori sat back in her chair. "Did you tell him?"

"What?"

"That you loved him, dummy."

Taylor shook her head, then grabbed a napkin and wiped her eyes. "I couldn't."

"Why not?"

"Because I'd buried myself in a hole. I'd told him in no uncertain terms that I hated living on the ranch. That I wanted nothing to do with the likes of him."

"He believed you?"

Taylor looked up at Frankie. "Why wouldn't he?"

"Because he's supposed to be a smart man."

"Gee, you're making me feel so much better."

Frankie shook her head. "Taylor, you have to tell him."

"No."

"So you're just going to give up? Leave with your tail between your legs? Come on, girl. You've fought for everything good that you have. Your education. Your job. Why stop now?"

She looked at Lori, then at Frankie. It was clear neither of them understood. "I can't," Taylor said.

"Yes, you can," Lori insisted.

"I'm afraid," Taylor said, humiliated to admit that she, the big brave sister who was always telling them to face their fears, was just a chicken. "He never once said he loved me. Even when we were..."

"Okay, fine," Lori said. "So he didn't say it. What if he's just as stubborn as you? What if he was waiting for you to say it first?"

"Zach's not like that."

"No? Did it ever occur to you that he might have wanted to ask you to stay, but that he didn't dare believe you'd want to?"

Taylor sniffed. "No."

"For a smart woman, you're not very bright." Lori took her hand. "Don't you know men are hopeless when it comes to this stuff? That for all their confidence, all their bravado, they're scared to death to admit they're in love? I had to propose to Jarred."

"And I was the one that told Cal I loved him, first."

"I don't know," Taylor said, wanting so much to believe them. But that was so risky. What if she got her hopes up again, and then found out they were wrong? That Zach really didn't want any women on his ranch or in his life?

"Let me ask you this," Lori said. "What's the worst thing that would happen if you told him you loved him?"

"He'd bust a gut laughing."

"Come on, be serious."

"The worst thing would be that he'd feel sorry for me."

"How much worse is that than what you have now?"

"At least now I can hope."

"That'll certainly be a comfort in your golden years," Lori said.

"Lori's right," Frankie said, her voice full of enthusiasm. "You really don't have anything to lose."

"Just my pride."

"Pride never kept a woman warm on a cold winter's night," Lori said.

Taylor sighed. "I'll think about it."

ZACH STOOD by the sliding glass door, staring out at the hot tub. He remembered her there, remembered the feel of her hands on his back. The look of her in her pretty bathing suit. He didn't want to think those things, but no matter how hard he tried, he couldn't stop it.

"Zach?"

He turned. Pearl was at the door of the kitchen. She

was in her nightgown and robe. He'd thought she'd been asleep for hours.

"Go to her, Zach."

"What?"

"You heard me. Don't let her go. You'll regret it all your life."

"She doesn't want what I have to offer," he said, not even trying to deny her assumptions.

"How do you know?"

"She told me."

"When?"

"About fifty times."

"Now, if you'd told me fifty-one, I'd say you were right."

"Come on, Pearl."

She walked toward him slowly. "Do you trust me?"

"You know I do."

"Then trust me about this. Go to her. Ask her to come back. Tell her how you feel."

"I can't."

"Zachary Baldwin, you're a lot of things, but I never thought you were a coward."

"Coward?"

"Yes. The worst thing that can happen is that she'll turn you down. You won't be any worse off if she does. But she won't."

"How do you know?"

"I just know."

He sighed, turning back to stare at the water in the hot tub. "I'll think about it."

"You do that. Honey, it's the rest of your life we're talking about."

"Pearl?"

"Yes?"

"What if she does come back, and then she hates it."

"Zach, she's not your mother. She won't leave like that. Couldn't you see that she was having the time of her life here? You're an observant man. Don't tell me you really didn't see that she was born to do this."

He nodded, wishing he could be that sure. Wondering if he had the guts to tell Taylor that despite his best intentions, he'd fallen in love with her.

TAYLOR SLOWED her horse down to a walk. She'd been riding hard, and she was afraid that she was wearing the poor girl out.

She had to call Quentin today. She couldn't put it off any longer. If she did, she'd lose the job. It wasn't fair, but all the enthusiasm she'd had about going to Washington had been lost on her trip to Wyoming. So now she didn't have the man she loved, and she didn't love the job she had.

Maybe she should just give in and call Zach. Lori and Frankie hadn't let up on her. Not yesterday, not this morning. She was actually starting to believe they might be right.

Even if they weren't, she couldn't go on like this. It would drive her crazy. She couldn't stop thinking about him. Not even in her dreams. Her mind played tricks on her, and she kept thinking that she heard him call. Or that she saw him in the distance.

She took a deep breath as she looked at the wide desert vista. So different from the mountains, yet beautiful in its own way.

If she took the job in Washington, she wouldn't be riding again anytime soon. She wouldn't be able to look up at the stars on a dark night and see the Milky Way. She wouldn't have to wake up at dawn. Or take care of a mangy herd of cows. No mucking out stalls, polishing leather.

She never should have gone to Wyoming. If she could turn back the clock, she would. Everything would be so much simpler. Every time she let herself care about someone, it all went to hell. It hurt like crazy to think she'd never see Zach again. The thought of that was what finally pushed her over the line.

She turned her horse around and headed back to Lori's house. She'd made her decision. She was going to call Zach. She was going to tell him everything, and then accept whatever he said. But no matter what, she wasn't going to go to Washington. She belonged here. On a ranch. Doing what she did best.

Now that she'd made up her mind, she wanted to get to it. If he told her no—which was what she expected—she wasn't going to hurt more than she already did. So what did she have to lose? At least this way, she'd have some closure.

She urged the horse on, wishing she hadn't ridden so far.

As she got closer to the ranch, she saw someone on a horse coming toward her. At first she thought it was Frankie, but then...

It was her mind playing tricks again. It had to be. Surely she couldn't be seeing Zach.

Yet the longer she stared, the more certain she became that she wasn't hallucinating. The way he sat in his saddle. The broadness of his shoulders. The way he wore his hat.

Her heart sped up so fast she thought she might pass out. He'd come for her! It couldn't be anything else. Why would he come all the way to Arizona just to tell her he didn't love her? It was too wonderful. Too incredible. She rode straight and fast, and grinned hard when she saw the dust his horse was kicking up. Evidently, he was in a hurry, too.

Finally he reached her, and before his horse had stopped, he flung his leg over in a running dismount. She scrambled down to meet him, and before she could utter a word, she was in his arms, and he was kissing her. Kissing her over and over, kissing her mouth, her cheeks, her eyes.

She was laughing and crying, trying hard to believe this was real, that he wasn't a dream.

"I can't let you go," he said. "Not when I love you so much. You don't have to work on the ranch. You can write, you can get a job with the paper. I can't give you Washington, but we've got a government in Wyoming. Would that do?"

She held his head in her hands and laughed again.

"No, it won't. Nothing will do but for me to be on that ranch of yours. As for your no-women-on-the-ranch business, honey—get over it. Because once I'm there, I'm not leaving. Not ever."

He gazed at her, and she gazed back, only now believing that it was real. That he loved her. She knew she'd been a fool for not telling him sooner.

"Are you sure? You know that it's not going to be an easy road."

"I know that. But being together will make it easier."

"I can be pretty damn stubborn."

"Really? Nah. I don't believe you."

"Cut it out, Taylor. This isn't funny. I'm serious."

She tried hard to wipe the smile off her face, but she couldn't. The feeling inside her, the pure pleasure of it all, made her want to sing at the top of her lungs. If he hadn't been holding her, she was sure she'd be ten feet off the ground. "I know, Zach. I know that you're stubborn, and that you get grouchy when you're hungry. I know that you don't like people to see how much you care about things. And I know that once you love, you love for keeps."

He nodded. "If you come back with me, I'll never let you leave."

"I know that, too."

"So, you'll marry me?"

She sighed, and said a silent thanks to whoever was watching over her. "Yes, Zach. I'll marry you."

His grin was the cherry on top. The icing on the cake. "I was thinking—" he said.

"Yes?"

"I was thinking that it might be nice to have a family."

She nodded. "A bunch of kids, huh? What if some of them are girls? What about your rules?"

"Well, I guess things will have to change. It'll be *our* playground. Not just mine anymore."

She couldn't keep still another moment. She just had to kiss him. With all the love in her heart. With all her hopes for their future.

Zach was her cowboy, and she wasn't ever going to let him go.

Look for a new and exciting series from Harlequin!

Two __new__ full-length novels in one book, from some of your favorite authors!

Starting in May, each month we'll be bringing you two new books, each book containing two brand-new stories about the lighter side of love! Double the pleasure, double the romance, for less than the cost of two regular romance titles!

Look for these two new Harlequin Duets™ titles in May 1999:

Book 1:
WITH A STETSON AND A SMILE
by Vicki Lewis Thompson
THE BRIDESMAID'S BET
by Christie Ridgway

Book 2:
KIDNAPPED? by Jacqueline Diamond
I GOT YOU, BABE by Bonnie Tucker

**2 GREAT
STORIES BY
2 GREAT
AUTHORS
FOR 1 LOW
PRICE!**

Don't miss it! Available May 1999 at your favorite retail outlet.

HARLEQUIN®
Makes any time special.™

Look us up on-line at: http://www.romance.net   HDGENR

COMING NEXT MONTH

#769 SUDDENLY A DADDY by Mindy Neff
Delaney's Grooms
Dylan Montgomery was the kind of man who could take anything on the chin. But when Dylan found one of Karl Delaney's infamous notes in his coat pocket that said he would be a daddy, a light breeze could have flattened Dylan. Because the only mommy could be...Karl's niece, Whitney Emerson.

#770 THE HUNK & THE VIRGIN by Muriel Jensen
Being stuck with gorgeous stud Gib London for six weeks was going to be torture for old-fashioned Kathy McQuade. The sexy bodyguard was supposed to be guarding her virtue—not tempting her to abandon it!

#771 THE MOST ELIGIBLE...DADDY by Tina Leonard
Sexy Single Dads
Noreen Cartwright's elderly relatives were on a mission: to get her off the shelf. Since the stubborn young woman wanted no time with a fella, the three ladies set to matchmaking her with Parker Walden—the sexiest man and most eligible daddy Rockwall, Texas, had ever seen!

#772 HOW TO CATCH A COWBOY by Karen Toller Whittenburg
Kurt McCauley had long been a thorn in Emily Dawson's side. But while the too-handsome, too-famous cowboy was pining for Emily's sister, he somehow wound up married to Emily! They'd just have to get an annulment—except, Kurt knew they'd had a wedding night. And might be having a baby...

Look us up on-line at: http://www.romance.net